GUERNICA NIGHT

D1320474

GUERNICA NIGHT

Barry N. Malzberg

NEW ENGLISH LIBRARY/TIMES MIRROR

In Memory of Gil Orlovitz: 1919-1973

'Therein the milky eclipse of the sun,
and no blindness; the roaring and we are not deaf;
and the acid, and we have not been eaten away.'

7 April, 11 pm.

First published in the USA in 1974 by Bobbs-Merrill Company, Inc.
First published in Great Britain in 1978 by New English Library

© 1974 by Barry N. Malzberg

First NEL Paperback Edition October 1979

NEL Books are published by
New English Library Limited from
Barnard's Inn, Holborn,
London EC1N 2JR.
Made and printed in Great Britain by
Hunt Barnard Printing Ltd.,
Aylesbury, Bucks.

45003556 5

CONTENTS

PROLOGUE

Here we are in Disney Land/Disney World. Disney Land or Disney World; hard to make the changes on these – one in California, the other in Florida – but the continent has become spliced, as we know, and Disney, God rest him at the age of sixty-five and through eternity, believed in the controlled and timeless environment, stripped of any conception of space. Disney was right. This is the concept that must be held at all costs, unless, of course, you hold that he is wrong, which is also a possibility. Right. Wrong. California. Florida. Here we are: this is the point.

Here we are in Disney Land/Disney World; clutching the strange hands of those with whom we came, we move slowly through the ropes under the chanting of the attendants, swatting at the insects of habitation, toward the exhibit of the martyred President. The martyred President has become a manikin activated by machinery, tubes and wiring; he delivers selected portions of his famous addresses, stumbling back and forth upon the stage, his plastic joints trembling off-rhythm, and this proves that history can be not only educational: it can be genuinely entertaining. There is a certain anxiety. It is near closing time, and we fear that the exhibit will be shut before it is our time to pass through the lines; how could we return to our homes, our friends, without being able to say that we have seen the exhibit of the martyred President? It is impossible for us to make this admission; we would be the laughingstock of the neighborhood if we admitted that we had gone to Disney Land/Disney World without seeing that for which he is most famous (having already ridden the monorail, which is a very distant second choice), but lying about it would be most difficult. We would be quizzed on details very closely, as are all returnees from the Disney exhibitions, and sooner or later our ignorance would be shown; we would stagger up against the recollection of one who knew better . . . and what then would there be to say? One can hardly come to grips with this.

The sky, a dense inverted bowl, falls tightly over the World or Land of Disney tonight. At all costs Disney wanted a controlled environment, but he was not able, up to the point of his death from cancer, to figure out a way to keep the atmosphere itself out; given a little more time, he would have worked out something . . . but now the air, laden with insects and small heat flashes, presses on us closely; for a moment there is that discommoded sense of a certain lurch toward collapse; irreality seems to embrace us . . . a small explosion of fatigue at the end of a long day. Not to think of it. The line is moving now, the attendants whisking us along, and just as we think that we will not get into the exhibit this time but will surely make it on the next, we are allowed through – the very last, in fact, of the throng to get in – and as we move through the ropes into the passageway the feeling of fatigue passes. It is impossible that we could have ever felt faint. It was merely the anticipation. Now that we are in, now that we are going to see the exhibit, that weak sensation goes away, and we sense little burbles of laughter beginning to move viscously inside. We feel fine. Everybody feels fine. Children are smiling. Over us is the smooth bulkhead of the building; the cooling climate system of Disney whisks its way through us. Strangers and family, friends and acquaintances jostle around us as we move down the ramp and into an auditorium, take a seat at a high place in the last row. We look through the auditorium and see that every face here is that of someone we know, if not from a long time ago, then from quick meetings in the corridors of the other exhibits. Nods are exchanged, little waves, greetings. Fingers prod at our hands, and we prod them back. The lights glisten, then fall away, and we are in the darkness. Far down on the stage the curtains part. The dead President shuffles forward. The dead President raises his hand. The dead President begins to move on the stage, side to side, and from behind him comes the sound of anthems. He greets us.

We listen to him. The darkness draws us together, and truly never have we felt so close; never have I felt so close – I must admit this – to myself, to some sense of the nation which joins me together as the President begins to speak. Phrases roll limpidly from him; his gestures are rather mechanical, but then again, bathed in the spotlight, his visage is very lifelike, his flesh of an excellent hue. The music rises. He continues.

Listening to him, we feel that we are on the verge of an insight; an insight so deep and strange, true and final that it will eclipse everything that we have known before, every portion of our lives, and in this attitude it is easy to understand Disney's genius as well; his ability to give us the past in a way that will become our future. And so, in perfect harmony, accord, we listen and listen, the little figure yanking itself around the stage and, as the rifle fire begins, leveling at his neck, then temple, in the old and accustomed way. It is with a sheer outcry of love that we watch him fall toward the stage as the cleansing fires begin . . . and the walls of the exhibit fall away from us; they dissolve utterly, leaving us in Disney Land/Disney World forever, and as the insects come over us, it is as if we too have become artifacts, the insects muttering secrets into our ears that will in turn activate us someday so that we, actors, may create new histories for the future.

PART I

DANCE

I

Accelerator to the floor: make the engine wail. From the tapes, I hear what seem to be the glossy sounds of copulation, although they are only – I must know this – songs from the past carrying me home. Down the abandoned corridor of 1-80 we whisk like bugs, Sherry and I, one of her little hands pressing the pit of my groin, the other raised to the panels of my cheek, her gracious teeth imprinting a pattern upon my earlobe which neatly augments, addresses those sounds, although it is difficult to separate impressions. Life is a totality. Like a great hunk of meat, it hangs loose and flapping against the wall of consciousness. Try to take out one part, examine it, and the blood spurts.

A rabbit, maddened as if in refraction of my own heat, scoots from one side of the road to the other. I pick him up for an instant in the lights, little steam vapors coming from the animal as he is locked into frieze; then, with a dull splat, a diminished and diminishing seventh of the spirit, I hit him, send the body spinning high to the grasses. It becomes another part of the dark.

Sherry shakes in her seat, catches her breath – frozen little bitch – and then exhales coolly, evenly, my eardrum baking to her temperature. The speedometer of the Cadillac is at seventy; a fair reading this: I have it calibrated for error at no more – no more, mind you – than five miles per hour out of the first sixty. The system worked out with the Cadillac up on blocks in the hidden enclosure, huffing gray at me, the vapors exciting. Once again she presses. The heat is building; my lust is atmospheric but no less real for all of that.

'Sid, oh, Sid,' she says. My wizened genitals respond to her pressure with a heartbeat of their own -- whisk, whisk, whisk under the tapestry of cover. 'Oh, Sid, you shouldn't have done it to that poor little thing,' and impulse seizes me, or perhaps it is merely some lyric poured from the radio, something about loving and craving. I jab on the brakes irrhythmically, the vacuum stoppers hissing, the car beginning to tremble into a long, slow glide, and then we are bouncing and rattling on the shoulder of I-80, the dead stones coming under the ornament of undercoat, devils slinging little pellets at the base of the car. In her gasp is astonishment. 'What are you doing?' she says. 'What are you doing to us now?'

Silly. Silly, silly, wretched little bitch, what does she think I am doing? But I conceal my tongue within the damp corridor of mouth even as her hand dodges, and the car – all two and a half tons of wasted, gnarled metal, a true and cunning artifact resurrected by *me* – settles to collapse on the side of the road. I extend a fist, then splay it into a hand, and bring her against me, feeling the thin steam again coming from a thousand pores of her body, her empty little breasts darting up and down my arm like insects. Always at the moment of imminence I am obsessed by scatological images; someday I will confide this to the Group.

'What do you think I'm doing?' I say. 'What do you think this is, anyway?' and cut the headlights instantly. Now we are in a dark, deep cubicle, some compartment of the spirit, the engine dead, the radio dead, my heart alive and filled with necessity. And I say, 'I'm going to take you, that's what I'm going to do,' feeling at once the treacherous contraction of her flesh as she moves from me, leaning now on the door opposite, her eyes two spots in the darkness. Momentarily I hit the transfer point and am deep within her head; I know exactly what is passing through her mind, and it is as if the words are imprinted on some teletype of the synapses. Fear, disgust, loathing, uncertainty fall against one another like clowns as the strips come from the teletype; holding them together is that bright red string

12

of mindless desire which controls her life. Which controls all of them, for truly, truly, they are receptacles and can be seen in no other way.

'No,' she is saying now. 'Sid, you can't do it; we can't do this now,' and that is all I need to hear. I am now inflamed, monstrous, leveled by strength – to say nothing of conviction – and I move across the seat on the pedestal of buttocks, feeling them jutting into the seat as though they were little legs carrying me home (I am liable to sudden lurches of insight such as this – it is a condition of my brooding, rather visual intelligence – but undue credence should not be placed in them), and my hands strike forward in impromptu salute: *one! two!* arcing to touch the dull planks of her shoulders, her body all wood and planes within my grasp; but no matter, no matter at all: she will soften yet.

'Ah,' she says, 'ah God, no,' and I seize a breast, touch it underneath the cloth; then, in a rending motion, tear her blouse aside and hold the other in my free hand. Her little hands twitch and flutter against the roof panels as I feel that turgid, familiar rising below, and then, at the moment of presumptive entry, there is –

– A sudden reversal of impulse, a falling away, contraction, woe and dead below the waist, my groin feels imploded as if slivers of metal had been pierced. It has all happened before. I hold myself in that frozen posture against the window, allowing her to bang and rattle against me. Suddenly not interested, my eyes turn to the now-accustomed dark, and I look out upon the vast, deserted plains of New Jersey, seeing imaginary curls of brown filth come from the stacks of refineries long departed, industry that now seems bucolic. Strange: it is strange, but at this moment of ultimate connection, I feel myself no longer to be a man but a machine, some creation of the departed age of technology dreaming amidst the loops and wires, the barrels and refuse of the culture.

'What's wrong?' she is saying. 'Sid, oh Sid, what's wrong with you now?'

Little bitch, I think, the little bitch was waiting for it all of the time; even her terror contrived, some necessity of the glands to heighten her own excitement, some outpouring keyed by metabolism to make her slicker, darker, hotter and emptier. And I say *Nothing*, jabbing against her, *Nothing is the matter*, my thighs moving emptily in some parody of the spasms of

13

intercourse, making their own dull comment . . . And I can see, moving close against her, that she is looking at me with interest and concern, with even a bit of awe. She must know that I am strong; she knows that I am really crazy, and I can see her add my newly discovered madness, another gleaming bead, to the rosary of her apprehension. She is working things out.

'Interstate 80 was abandoned hundreds of years ago,' I say, pieces of the tapes coming back to me. 'The federal highway lobby fell apart. Mass transit temporarily replaced the old private means of access; the passenger automobile was outlawed. Interstate 80 is planked over in most of the country; that which isn't has weeds. This is one of the few sections that still exist, probably illegally, and we are driving in one of the last operable automobiles of our sector. We are alone. No one has the means to find us. We could not be detected by search parties for days; it is just the two of us, lost out here.'

I have said this, I think, to excite her, but there is no response. I continue mindlessly. 'We are an artifact on an artifact,' I say; 'we perform the anachronism of connection in a wasteland where connection truly does not exist.' There is a little twitch, and, rising now, I feel it.

'In the old days, people used to go out in motor cars to do this,' I point out. 'People like us, people of our age, did not have units of their own, quarters in which to mate. Mating was important to them, however, and so they were compelled to go out in pairs or quarters in motor cars to fashion the instant of copulation amidst layers of steel and glass, plastic and rubber. We have been reconverted to our past. We have become our past. We *are* the past, you silly bitch.'

And now, even as she gasps, I am tumescent, excited. 'Come here,' I say then. 'Come here to me.'

'Sid,' she says, 'oh, Sid, you're crazy, you really are,' as I drop my hands once more to her breasts, ringing them like bells, their gong and clatter pouring through the car, the sound of their ringing enchanting me, another anachronism. Enormous, fully potent, I corner her against an armrest, yank at her skirt and pull her hands toward me to pull me through, to assist in the difficult task of conjoinment. For all of our desire, I have decided that it is really not a natural act, not at all: like the workings of machinery itself, it comes from certain pressures and tensions cunningly applied.

'Come on,' I say. 'Come on, now,' beginning to grunt like

14

a pig in the swill of excitement . . . and perhaps she assists me, perhaps she does not; it is difficult to be quite sure of this in the welter of increasing sensation. All that I know is this: something long and porous springs from me, something with many holes and openings which needs fulfillment, and somehow in the clustered space of the car then it *is* filled. Those empty, aching, groaning spaces are suddenly overtaken by a clear substance which plugs me up; strange and ominous reversal, since, as far as I know, it is the woman who is filled, the man who has access in the actions of intercourse; but then –

– Oh well, I have always had homosexual elements – all of us do; why deny them? – and they are working in the compound here. In any event, here I am on 1-80 in a ruined Cadillac, taking another round of passion, hard to tell, hard to tell indeed exactly what this is going to lead to, although I am willing to partake of whatever may happen. Experience, then, is its own reward: I am willing to make this golden, shrinking pursuit, just as I was willing to seek its very initiation on the dull, darkened corridors of 1-80, and this insight comforts me. It does indeed, homosexual tendencies or not; it becomes a wedge to lever me from my own darkness as I ring the bells –

– And the sound of bells is all around me, filling the air with its density and perfume. There we are, purring like dangerous animals against each other, entering and reentering the opened engines of self as the fog rolls in and the ignition of the dead car ticks out counterpoint to the sound of the insects, until I penetrate her to her deepest point.

And this, then, is but one of the events of one of the days; there are many others, to be sure, many other occurrences, and it would be wrong to consider this even as a metaphor, for it is not. It is merely a simple bit of love-making, as almost anyone who has ever performed it should know.

II

Later there is the dangerous business of sliding the old car into its hiding place without detection. Sherry, in the aftermath, has become giddy; little giggles burst from her open lips like dribbles of saliva from the overdosed, and her body shakes under the blanket. 'Quiet, bitch, quiet,' I say, pushing the snorting length of the car into the blocks beckoning to hold it, but her laughter increases, and I am forced to hammer in the foot brake, turn and hit her across the face once, hard, bringing white in the creases from which the blood has retreated, and then her head cracks against the power window; she is sobbing as I continue my task, squeezing the unresilient metal like a loaf of bread into the sheath. At overheat the dial swings dangerously; I smell the odors of corruption within the car. Finally it is done and we sit in the enclosure, a perfect darkness overtaking, and I look at her. She has ceased sobbing, is sitting stunned under the blanket in a posture of tenderness, and I am overtaken suddenly by a feeling of tenderness so profound that it might be mistaken for compassion if I did not know the difference.

'Stop it,' I say, 'stop it,' and slide over the seat to hit the door release, prying open the button, and the door falls away, opening into the enclosure, a single shaft of light pinning her, stricken madonna, on the seat. 'Get out,' I say. 'Get out now.'

'Oh, Sid,' she says, 'Sid, you do not understand; you understand nothing.'

'I understand all of it,' I say. 'I understand what is necessary,' and jab my fist into her thigh. Slowly then she begins to move, beating like a heart in the blindness, and finally she is out of the car. I come out on her side, panting. The two of us stand for a moment in that emptiness, seeing nothing, and then I feel the touch of her hand seeking mine. I feel overwhelmed by a sensation I cannot give a name. She makes that contact; we stand there in the strangeness, and for a moment I feel that I have understood something, but I know as always that this will go away, and all, in the morning, will be as it has been before.

'What will you do if they find your car, Sid?' she says to me in the fields outside the complex.

'I will get myself another one, then,' I say.

'But what will you do if you cannot get another?'

'I will do what is necessary,' I say, and she laughs swiftly in the cold lights from the complex, turns to kiss me like a moth, and then is gone. Slowly, I turn toward the place of my own devising.

III

Later, or perhaps this on a different day – it is hard to say; everything blurs together – I have a dream, and in this dream I am visited at bedside by Ludwig van Beethoven (1770–1827) and John F. Kennedy (1917–1963). I am often haunted by similar figures from the imagined or real past; the celebrated dead have made my cubicle a listening post. Beethoven and Kennedy appear to have been engaged in intense conversation before they entered the cubicle, something to do, perhaps, with the many similarities between political manipulation and the composition of the choral symphony, both of them exercises in megalomania, absolute control of the ideal, something like that anyway, and the conversation must have been good-humored, perhaps even festive, because both of them are in high good spirits, giving each other many private nudges and chuckles, Kennedy cackling away, Beethoven in good humor . . . because, although they turn serious when they see me, it is a false attempt, almost as if they were acting out of a sense of obligation, because all of the celebrated dead with whom I deal are here on solemn missions and attempt to furnish me with guidance and a good example.

Still, as they settle in, it is easy to see that didactic elements are not foremost in their minds. More than anything, Beethoven and Kennedy seem to want to leave the room to continue their often scatological conversation. 'In time, gentlemen,' I say to them obscurely – they do not understand what I am saying, of course – 'in time you will.'

'Nevertheless,' Kennedy says unresponsively, 'nevertheless, you are wasting your life,' jabbing his forefinger in that characteristic way which I recollect from the old tapes. Kennedy also had a brother – two brothers; one of them was also killed, but I cannot approach this material now. For that matter, there is a respectable school of thought holding that the brothers, even the one who was killed, are merely an extension of the myth: one Kennedy is not enough for us; one death too inexplicable; therefore there must be a doubling; but I am not sure of this. Beethoven is also a mystery, although I do know about the symphonies.

'You must be disciplined,' Kennedy continues. 'You must gain control of the elements of your life; you must put them together. You must remember that our time on Earth is limited, but in that brief span there is much to accomplish.'

'Is there?'

'Oh, indeed, *much* to accomplish; wouldn't you agree with that, Ludwig?' he says with just a trace of uncertainty, turning then to Beethoven, and Beethoven, the warts on his pock-marked face congealing in some explosion of eagerness, or perhaps it is only deep thought, says, 'Yes, that is exactly true. Wouldn't you think that I of all people could attest to that? Our time is indeed limited, and also, syphilis lurks to corrupt the incautious.'

His eyes wink and blink away in compulsive patterns; his frockcoat, infested with small foreign lice, sways as he gestures vigorously. There is no trace of accent in Beethoven's voice, which is surprising, since I had expected there would be. But there are certain imponderables in all of these dream-dialogues, and I am in no position to say whether or not they have much basis in reality. I am fully aware at all times that this is a construction, of course. 'Indeed,' Beethoven says, 'of course, quite, very definitely, much to accomplish, no doubt about it,' and he nods vigorously.

The nod unsettles his balance; unlike Kennedy, the musician does not seem to be at the peak of physical condition as he staggers against a wall, the tails of his coat flapping. 'Besides,' he says, 'it's not only a matter of wasting your life; John is quite right about that, but you're wasting the lives of everyone you're having dealings with. Instead of being for them the person that you could be now, and bringing out the best in them, what you're doing is making them *worse*,' and his head begins to jerk, one insane convolution upon the next, the twitches piling together in a way to make him seem quite energetic, although I know that this is not the case: actually he is suffering from dropsy, as I recall from our last interview.

Even though I have no inkling of what Beethoven is talking about, he, at least, seems enormously pleased with himself. If I did not know all through that this was a dream and that both K and B (as I will subsequently refer to them in a shorthand of the spirit, dreams enabling one to splice information and reassemble it in quite a cunning way) were reconstructions of my faulty retrospection, existing patches from scraps of knowl-edge, popular impressions, the image of film; even if I did not know this, I would still take their protestations with doubt, be-

18

cause a sense of certainty was drained out of our lives at about the time that the unfortunate K was killed. This much at least is clear.

'And anyway,' K says, leaning back against the wall in a contrived posture which does not quite conceal, try as he may, the trembling of his left hand as he slips it into a pocket, the accusing shake of fingers which always belied him at critical instants, ' – anyway, what you did with that girl on 1-80, Interstate 80 I mean, was absolutely inexcusable. We can't go along with something like that, Sid.'

'What's that?'

'You raped her,' K says. 'You very definitely raped her, Sid. Anyone could see that.'

'I did not rape her.' I stand, agitated. 'She was cooperating, pleading, in fact. There was nothing at all forcible about it.'

K gives me one of his shyest and best smiles. 'You most certainly did,' he says. 'In the society from which I come, in the code of conduct which I accept as a gentleman, any entrance of the female without her full and final consent is rape.'

'You understand nothing,' I say. 'You understand nothing at all, not even the mechanics.'

'In Vienna,' B says reminiscently, crouching on the floor, ' – in Vienna this was not entirely true. It is well known that many of my affairs were scurrilous and ill managed. Still, which of us is qualified to pass judgment – '

'*I* am,' K says sternly. I can sense that their relationship, so amiable up until now, may be showing little signs of strain. 'There are certain prerogatives, certain judgments which are constant and understood. This would be one of them.' He gives B quite a menacing glare.

'I wasn't going to say a thing,' B says mildly enough. 'I was just listening.'

'Don't interrupt, in any case. I'm trying to straighten out Sid here, show him the ways of discipline and force before his indolence undercuts him totally.'

'What would you know of Vienna?' B says petulantly, but he rubs his palm together with a hip in a defeated gesture and slinks against the bed, as I, by some counter-action, spring to my feet, begin to pace quite restlessly. In certain ways this dialogue has shaken me, but in other ways, more profoundly, it has not. I am quite aware that all of it is imaginary, and at this point I would like it to stop.

'Pardon me,' I say, trying to keep up my part of the conversation, a certain bantering lightness which will avert open hostility, get them out of here, ' – pardon me, but as you know I was resting when you came in. Unless you have anything more to say, then, I'd really appreciate – '

'There's a great deal more to say,' K says briskly, putting a ghostly hand on my shoulder and pushing me to the bed. I collapse on the slats, narrowly missing an elbow in B's eye, and fall back into the wall. 'There's a great deal to be understood if only you would listen.'

Fascinated, regarding him from this angle, I think that I am able to see the small scar left by the entrance of the second bullet, a healed line stretched in cross-patching across the back of his neck, that line sealing the skin into an imprecise parody of a mouth that might at any instant split open to gape, produce a tongue to run through that space reminiscent of a kiss. 'You must pick up on your history,' K says. 'You must make a more dedicated effort to function in your survival group, and you must cease to spread your seed emptily and casually but should understand that sex, which is the production of life, is as sacred as life itself, the two of them intertwined, then – '

But this is quite enough. My lassitude has vanished. In fact, I spring from the bed, put hands on K's shoulders, guide him toward the door. For all that he is a specter, his flesh seems quite substantial, although quite thin and wasted, as would be the case, considering the disastrous ravages not only of the great Rifleman but of the worms beneath the Eternal Light. 'Enough of this,' I say. 'You have got to get out of here.'

K resists me weakly; his body flutters in my hands like a bird, much as Sherry's did the night of our recent (forced, I reluctantly agree) copulation. And I wrench K toward the door. 'Don't tell me about vigor!' I shout. 'Don't tell me about circumstances. Concentrate on your own disasters, you fool. Look first to Dallas! That's what you should be concerned about!' and similar admonishments. Quite easily K submits to my attack. He is physically weak, it seems, despite all of the sentiment and myth which has been shoveled through his damaged corpus, and he goes through the door easily, shrugging his shoulders, not precisely resisting but in fact collaborating in the moment of eviction.

'Don't come back!' I shout as he weaves in the hall. 'You're

20

not welcome here. I've had quite enough of this,' and slam the door on the stammering, humiliated, apologetic, helpless K — there is nothing like death to reduce the elements of power in a personality — and turn then to see that B has risen in a posture of attention, is looking at me out of the corners of his ravaged Viennese eyelids. Only the faint light which peeps from behind gives indication of intelligence.

'You too,' I say. 'Exactly the same applies to you. Get out of here now.'

'Ah,' B says quietly, raising his hands as if to fend off imminent attack, 'ah, there's no need for this, my friend. We simply came to give you counsel.'

'Get out.'

'I was deaf through the composition of my last seven symphonies, you know. I only got good when I became deaf. Before then I was distracted by so much going on outside of me, but once I became deaf, it was possible for me to exist as if I were the only voice in the world. Of course my hearing is perfectly restored now,' he adds, reaching into a pocket and taking out a pair of pince-nez which he clamps like nails to the bridge of his nose. His eyes, magnified, glare at me luminous, yet strangely placid, like fish. 'We're only trying to help you, Sid,' B points out. 'Your conduct has been disgraceful.'

'I don't know what to say,' I answer, and indeed I do not; throwing K out of the room seems to have exhausted my arsenal of retaliation. 'I really wish you'd leave.'

'Stealing cars from the repository; taking innocent girls out on the highways; committing yourself to enter their fair, firm and weak little bodies; misapplying your great talents; using yourself not to expand but to diminish . . . we merely wished to set an example for you. But then again,' B adds meditatively, much as if he were responding to some inner voice, 'it is quite true that we are hardly in a position to stand judgment upon you.'

I shake my head, retreat. The man is monomaniacal; there is no question about this. It would be hard to have anyone witness my position, but I am almost confident of the result; it would be seen that I have nothing for which to feel apologetic.

'K has made dreadful mistakes of his own which we won't go into at this time,' B continues, 'and my own life is an example of dissipation. All that syphilis and sublimated homosexuality. Very well, Sid,' B says, raising an admonitory palm before I can reach out to strike him. Really, I am quite disconcerted, there is no way in which I can sufficiently express the essential affront that this invasion, even if imagined, has been to my dignity. 'Very well,' B says, like all dream objects showing alertness toward the shifting of my moods. 'Very well, I won't continue. I can see that it's quite hopeless.'

He picks up the hem of his frockcoat in a strangely delicate gesture – quite feminine this; he might be a girl brushing past me quickly in exit from the Group; Sherry herself has never deserted me with such grace – and heads toward the door, leaving me standing with fists clenched at sides. I do not know now how to deal with him.

'It's your life, you see,' B says. 'You're living inside it, and we're hardly in a position to change it. But you should understand,' B says, ' – you should understand that K and I have had some very difficult times, have suffered for our failures, and what is the purpose of a past if you can't learn from it?'

'To be entertained.'

'To be entertained? No, Sid, there's no point in chronology at all unless we can assume that it magnifies into tradition, and tradition is there for knowledge. If you do not learn from what we have to tell you, Sid, then it is as if we never lived at all, and that's pretty humiliating; you understand that, Sid?'

And the thing is that I do, I really do follow what B is trying to say, but it is too late and too long – no time for any of this, and more immediate and pressing problems bearing in – so I merely place my hands deep into the damaged and insubstantial small of his back and propel him through the open door, pitching him from the room much as I had pitched K. There is a little shriek from the hallway as B collides with something, either K or a wall, and then K's whimper in the distance.

But enough. Enough of both of them. They are dead. I close the door and lean my back against it, breathing harshly, deeply. It is really bad enough to be the victim of the past, the unwitting, helpless outcome of history, let alone having to deal with these urgent and quarrelsome manifestations. I am only twenty; I have the Final Trip on my mind. Conflicts such as this could push me over; Sid could essay the Final Trip, and then where would he, to say nothing of his song, be?

Still on the lip of that dream I returned to the bed, and in the dream it is as if I collapse into yet a further sleep which superimposes upon all of this a dream of waking, a dream in which I come to the clear, bright spaces of the night alive and intent upon every pulsation of the darkness. There, in the center of the room, K and B are continuing their inexhaustible conversation, but now it is in a different language, and I can sense none of it. None of it whatsoever . . . and so I clamber into sleep, pure and clean this time without the knife strokes of the dreams drawing the blood of circumstance from my brain –

– And there I lie until midshift, when it is time once again to emerge from the porous spaces of the bed to face the Group, the tasks, the clamorous machinery of the day.

Sometimes I wonder about my life. I really, really wonder.

IV

In the Group later, Jag says that he is disgusted with his life and is disgusted with all of life as he knows it and that he cannot put up with it any longer and he will not deal with it any further, and so, at last, he is going to Final Trip. He will Final Trip just as soon as he can prepare himself psychologically for the jolt, which he does not think in any case will be three or four shifts hence. The important thing, as he states, is that he is going to do it. He has passed the point of decision.

Jag's face as he says this is truly impressive. I have never seen him so taken with himself. It coalesces past creases, and his eyes reveal a darkness and intelligence which would never have been suspected until he began talking about his Final Trip.

'I mean, I have considered it,' he says. 'I have looked here and there, up and down, and I see no reason to deny the ultimate. This is a decision which each of you must make on your own, of course . . . but speaking personally, I've never been happier.'

I had never heard anyone announce a Final Trip before. Corpses are common – discovered bodies in the halls, dangling from planks, lying in the grasses or dust outside in the mornings; it is not uncommon to see three or four a week. It is a rare week that passes indeed in which I do not see casual, offhand death, which never fails to be exciting. But I have never, until Jag, heard anyone announce prior intention. That is simply because no one in our curious Group ever has; a strange percentage. Under the tenets of the Group, of course, intention to F.T. must be stated at least one session before the action is taken, so that, nominally, the subject is given a chance to reconsider through argument. Other than the exposure to argument, there are no penalties; indeed, subversively, I have sometimes wondered if the F.T. might even be encouraged at some level as a means of easing the more ambitious from the population code.

The announcement, of course, being the first in the Group, is sensational. Immediately, the attempts at dissuasion commence.

'Don't do it,' Peter says. 'There's no reason to F.T.; after all, you haven't even lived. Have you, Jag? Can you make a decision on the basis of what you don't know?' But Jag merely nods and glares down the line, his mouth twitching in an involuntary *next* as I point out, 'There's no return from F.T., Jag. I wouldn't do it unless I were absolutely sure.'

'I am,' he says. 'I am absolutely sure. This is my decision and I've taken it very seriously.'

We have shared many good times together in and out of the Group, and indeed on the very night that I took Sherry out on 1-80, I offered her first to Jag as a measure of feeling for him, telling him that she was primed for sex and that he could do it as easily as I if only he were inclined. I have quite a high regard for him, in short. Nevertheless, in the Group, the hierarchies are defined, and special pleading cannot be invoked.

'If you want to do it, I guess you should just go ahead,' Sherry says. 'I mean it's up to you, isn't it?'

'That's right.'

'No one can stop you, right?'

'Not a chance.'

'It's just knowing that you've considered it. What I mean to say is that you've got to be absolutely sure. Is it something you really want to do? You shouldn't do something like this foolishly, unless you've given it a lot of thought.'

Sherry is not very bright, but there is no avoiding the dank little messages her fingernail traces in my palm. Square and crucifix, it goes; crucifix and square: she is saying that we are at peace again, that she has surmounted all doubt, and that if I show the proper regard for her future, I may make love to her again. She has decided that she enjoys that arcane activity. This knowledge, its impact driving a lever through the consciousness, distracts me from the next contributions: Susan's, Claire's, Ronald's and Billo's recommendations pass through and around me; I cannot make note of them. They are there to be picked up in the tapes later if I so desire, but I know that I will never do so, having been so excited by Sherry. I flash back her messages to her, turning her back upon herself in that way that women find exciting, giving a little touch here, a twitch there, until her palm becomes moist and begins to circulate around mine, winding in patterns like a snake. I can feel the heat coming from that joining; little beads of damp fall like jewels to the glowing surfaces of the floor and instantly evaporate, leaving a little shimmering prism in the air through which the lamps fluoresce. I am sure at this point that what we are doing is seen and look up frantically to see that it is not. Jag's decision has quite placed exclusive attention on himself (which is what he probably wanted), and now our leader himself is speaking directly to Jag, Jag's head still lowered, his eyes impassive but pleased.

Traditionally in the Group the leader has the first statement and the last, which is as it should be, of course, except that in the case of many leaders this is little more than a courtesy and they have nothing to contribute.

It is different with ours, however, whose name I do not know. It is not allowed, the naming of names; that is, until the elaborate ceremony that marks our expulsion from the Group years from now, too far to even demand curiosity. I have always thought that our head would have been someone interesting in the naming. He has a subtle message of great value to impart, if only we had the patience to truly attend him (but who does?), and now he is looking at Jag sadly as he says, 'The Final Trip is an evasion.'

'Is it?'

'You understand that as well as I do, Jagway.'

'That's just government shit,' Jag says, looking at the floor; 'that's what they tell you to say. It isn't an evasion of anything.'

'Yes, it is.'

'What then?'

'Of responsibility, of course. Of our great need to remain human in this world, no matter what the difficulty.'

'That's all a lot of bullshit out of the capital. They're sorry that they're past twenty-five and made the mistake of trying to live.'

25

'No, it's a denial of our humanity,' the leader says, somewhat confused. 'We have got to affirm our humanity, not deny it.'

'I don't give a shit about confirmation,' Jag says. 'I've reached this decision. It's a good one and it's mine, and I'm not going to have it changed at all.'

Still, I can sense that there is sullen and defensive nature in his voice now. My original reaction to his statement, a great vaulting gasp of elation and discovery, is already being tamped down: is it possible that Jag was not sincere, that he can be argued out of this? I realize that I passionately want to believe in the solidity of his decision; I do not want him to be changed, never knowing, until it is later stated in the Group how badly I need an F.T., perhaps as a measure of testing my own responses against it. For a long time I have thought about it, have pushed myself against the edge of that possibility, but I am not ready, I have not yet been ready to elect . . . I am only twenty years old, after all. There is still plenty of time in which to elect.

Still, I can understand the leader's problem as well. Whenever the very serious issue of the F.T. is raised, his instructions (I have checked their instructions in my own tape access; they are freely available to anyone who would think of requesting their *modus operandi*) are to try to counter it on every level, to check it for seriousness, to make the depth of intention stand clear. He is merely the 'leader' according to his instructional tapes; that is only how he may be defined to us. Presumably, when the remainder of us reach the end of training, he will, according to all the tradition I understand, reveal his name, his identity to us in an informal session; but I am not curious. He has no revelations for me. He cannot be much older than twenty-eight, but twenty-eight is quite old under all the conditions – three years past the Year of Last Option – and I feel very little sympathy for him, although a fair amount of the respect called for.

'You can't stop me,' Jag says. 'No one can stop me, because that's what I want to do. Now I just have to figure out the best time to do it.'

Sherry traces a little cube into my hand, listening; then with a fingernail she begins to prong at it. I find this unbearably exciting, particularly looking at the remoteness of her face, which seems wholly unattached to this action, giving no acknowledgment whatsoever. My genitals stir.

'You cannot be stopped from doing it if you insist,' the leader says.

'Of course. I know that.'

'The F.T. is a legitimate option; it is a fair choice, and under the common regulations it is quite within your power to execute and administer at any time that you desire.'

'I know that too. I know everything. I've studied up on this.'

'Still, the question of qualification is very strong. Have you thought about it?'

'Yes.'

'Do you believe that this is the only alternative you have?'

'Oh, very definitely,' Jag says softly. 'Oh yes, indeed I do.'

'Are you absolutely convinced that this is the only response you can make under the circumstances?'

'Yes again.'

The ritual of interrogation is strong and the leader merely working within practice as he goes through socratic process, but nevertheless I can sympathize with Jag. Perhaps his resolution was not that strong; perhaps he could use a little reinforcement. 'Go on,' I say to him. 'Go on and do it; don't listen to him. It's all a pack of shit anyway.' I squeeze Sherry's watery hand. 'Don't let anyone talk you out of what you know to be right.'

Jag looks at me gratefully as the leader begins to swear quietly. Still, this is within my rights; comments from the Group are not proscribed, and I have as much of a right to urge Jag forward as the leader does to try to hold him back. 'You're right,' Jag says, standing. 'It's all a pack of crap.'

'I'll say.'

'You go on, you mess around with your head, you live in a stinking four by four, and then they tell you to go out into the world and take the long trip. Damn it, I'd rather do it my way. The F.T. is a good deal; almost everyone does it.'

'Right,' I say. 'Right?'

'Sid,' the leader says, 'shut up.'

'You can't tell him to shut up,' Sherry says. 'He's got a right to speak.'

'You keep quiet too,' the leader says loudly. The Group, amazingly, seems on the verge of dissolution: there is the sense of fragmentation associated with spinning apart; but strangely it is Jag who saves it. He spreads his arms in approved

Crucifixion posture and we huddle, even the leader.

'Listen here,' Jag says. 'It's my decision, not anyone else's. There's no need to get excited, is there?'

'I'm not excited,' Sherry says. 'I just don't think we should fight.'

'No one's fighting,' the leader says. He runs a hand through his hair, focuses on the floor, grunts. 'Of course not,' he says. 'This is not within my province. No one can stop you.'

'Right,' Jag says, dropping his arms. 'That's right. No one can stop me.'

'But we are entitled to question. We are entitled to verify – '

'Don't question,' Jag says. 'Don't verify.' Standing, he looks at me, his hands clamped against his sides, his body swaying. 'You're right, Sid. It's all a pack of shit.'

'You know it,' I say. 'You know it.'

'All of you know it,' Jag says. 'All of you know it as well as I do, and although I may be the first, I won't be the last,' and he turns that gaze on us, his new way of looking, confronting each in a challenging way: softly at Sherry (he had wanted, I knew, to take her; it was merely fear); harshly at me, for we both knew the pain of life; soft again to Billo; and then penetratingly at Claire, with whom, I now see, he has coupled many times (it was *not* fear but grace which led him to turn down Sherry). 'Are any of you going to do it also?' he asks. 'Are any of you others going to declare? Are you big enough to take the F.T.?'

No one says anything. Claire coughs behind her hand, the hand unfurling like a handkerchief. Billo spits on the floor.

'All right,' Jag says. 'I see what kind of Group we've got here. Forget that I asked.'

'Jagway,' the leader says, 'that is enough of this. You are not permitted to encourage – '

'Forget that I asked,' Jag says. 'You can hold onto your miserable lives, for all the good that they do, but once you see me going down the chute, the rest of you are going to follow, and that's something you know yourselves. Once there's one F.T. in a Group, the whole Group suicides out; they aren't fools.' He turns toward the leader. 'I'm checking out,' Jag says, 'right now.'

'Look here – '

'The manual says I have to state it and you have a right to discuss it with me, but once I make the decision, I'm excused

28

from the Group until I do it – or until I change my mind and come back, and then I can't do it again. Isn't that right?'

Stricken, the leader nods. 'Yes,' he says, 'that's right.'

'So there's nothing more to say,' Jag says. He casts us the look again, less challenging this time, more pain and searching in it, and then walks to the door, opens it, and walks through, stands in that space for a moment. 'Are you going to stop me?' he says, and I see the desire in his eyes; seeing it, everything comes clear, if only momentarily, and I lunge toward him, some instinctive quiver of the flesh, retained only at the last instant, holding in check, then folded back into the seat slowly. I feel the hand within mine, clutching, and rage goes away. I feel weakened. 'Stop me,' Jag says. 'Come on, stop me.'

The leader shakes his head, runs a hand through his hair, focuses on the floor, then grunts. 'Of course not,' he says.

'Of course not.'

'That is not within my province. That is in no one's domain. But we do have the right to question you on – '

'Don't question,' Jag says. 'Do not, never, question; merely seize the choices.' He pauses. 'I'm going to do it, then,' he says. 'That's the end of it.'

He turns his gaze toward us, looks at each of us in that forbidding way, soft, hard, intermediate, soft and hard again, and then ends at Claire, looking deeply, her body coiling and uncoiling on the floor in the instinctive rhythms of sex. 'Are any of you with me?' he says. 'Claire? Billo? How about you, Sid? Have you had enough of the shit? Are you ready to take the Final Trip?'

I feel a chill and thrill, bump and smack along the groin but say nothing, pass under his gaze like a fish swimming into a deep net and then it is beyond. 'I knew it,' he says. 'I know the time will come. First me, and then the rest of you will follow.'

'No,' Sherry murmurs. 'No, we will not.'

'But of course you will,' Jag says. 'You'll find out what your lives mean after I've done it. I'm going. I'm going to F.T. out of this right now,' and I know that this is a lie, purely for effect; he would not conceivably do it at this time, but for all of that the effect has been massive. I know that none of us will ever be the same again. Jag leaves; the door flaps like a hand in the corridor damp, then hangs in the center. We stir uncomfortably and then turn toward the leader. He will tell us, we are thinking. He will tell us what this means, lend perspective, teach us that Jag is an aberration.

'Well,' he says, 'ah, well – ' and then hits a dangling pause of futility; we begin to move more restlessly, and I understand that he will have nothing more to say. He has nothing to add, sits there rigid in place. It is an embarrassment for the session to have reached this point of confrontation, but then everyone, the leader most of all, knows that Jag is well within his rights under all of the post-modern statutes and has merely done what would have been permitted any of us in his place. The air is damp, oppressive, circling in with fingers.

Sherry leans against me, and the heat pours off in little waves. I could insert my finger into her spirit, feel the aqueous damp, slide my fingers into the depths of her without opposition, so great her excitement, but I hold myself in place instead, unmoving, locking my frame. For the moment the knowledge is enough: she has become dangerously excited by Jag's declaration. Indeed, that sudden burst of water within may be attributed less to me than to my presence as surrogate for Jag, who is embarked upon deeper mysteries.

I should have seen this immediately, should have known it even before I felt the heat, but I cannot be blamed, I think, for having misunderstood in the light of this sudden revelation. I coil against her, trying to conjure feeling, but it will not work. There is nothing; it is only lust. I will have to settle for lust or nothing.

'I think,' the leader says finally, ' – I think we should go on now to discuss other matters. The nominal topic was political coefficients, and if we could move on then from there – '

But it is too late.

Too late, too late: half of life is that, and almost all of the rest too early. Already Billo has come to his feet, shuffling in place, making gestures toward the door; and as he does so, Claire rises, takes his elbow, and they look at each other in a strange way. Then Ronald is up, Susan as well; Sherry begins a battery of palm twitches which, mounting to metronomic rate, palpate their own urgency, and I am upright then, helping her courteously to her feet; and all of us, meeting at the door, confront the leader with stares so mysterious that he takes them as embarrassment.

'This is highly irregular,' he says at last, 'to cancel out a session this early. We should discuss; we should remain. We could drop the scheduled topic if you would prefer, and perhaps you would want to talk about the Final Trip. If any of you have thoughts, if you'd like to contribute – '

'No,' I say then. 'No. No Final Trips.'

'All right,' he says, and in this I can see the edges of his total capitulation. 'All right then. You're dismissed.'

'Thank you,' I say gravely. It seems that I have moved into a leadership vacuum. 'We're very appreciative.'

'But you'd be making a terrible mistake,' he says, bringing his palms together, 'just a very serious mistake if you were impressed by Jagway's declaration.'

'Who is impressed?' I say. The others are already leaving, except for Sherry, whom I am hanging onto despite her feeble attempts to join them. 'I'm not impressed. Are you impressed?'

'The Trip,' he says, 'I mean the Final Trip, is a very serious thing.' He stares up from his papers; his eyes glint a hint of sheer madness. 'It is a very sick thing. It used to be called suicide – '

'Two out of three do it,' I say. 'There's got to be something in it, no? More do it than don't.'

'*I* didn't do it.'

'Maybe you wish you had,' I say softly. 'Maybe that's what you mean, that you wish you had,' and this is a dart to the heart, a shot to the pot, pure vitriol to the brain, and he seems to crumple. Sherry tugs me toward the door.

'It's a sin,' he says weakly. 'Can't you understand that? It's a very terrible mortal sin,' and continues to babble, something about religiosity, but I lose the thread of it, and suddenly I am interested no more. It is impossible to take him seriously. Sherry guides me through. 'Jagway is setting a very bad example,' I hear the leader say, but it is quite too late, too late by far for any of this. We are in the corridors now, and I can feel the hard, hot, congealing lump of my erection bursting the cords of fabric as I stagger through the corridor, linked to Sherry, who transports me as if she were all motion in the world. We move toward the coupling room, only two kilometers down, the coupling room in which she will bring me to light, and I must smile inwardly, because this is the first time, the very first, that she has discarded subterfuge. At some perilous instant we bump against each other in the hall, and

31

her back feels like a pair of wings, soft, fluttering against my chest.

She is very excited, and I am excited as well, although it is difficult to understand this. I know the Final Trip well; have considered it many times; have discarded it because I did not think that the time was right. Why is Jag's decision heroic, whereas my willingness to temporize is without merit? But of course, of course: it is always those who seize the obvious who become heroes; it could have happened in no other way.

I do not blame her for this; I understand. In her position I might have done the same.

So we go to the coupling room then, linked together through the charge of our knowledge . . . and if this be the only way that we can break the shackles of our deprivation, if this be the only way that I can know her, then so be it. So be it. I will take what I can.

Inside, the taste of her vaults to my mouth like blood.

V.

But later, keyed to depression, I take the Transporter. Has Jag done what I did not have the courage to do? Has some vital part of myself been lost because it was he, not I, who declared first for the Final Trip? Pouring into the Transporter, easing myself through limbs first, the least frightening way as I have been instructed, I do not know, or know any of the sense of it at all. But it is depression, not Cage Process, which carries me through the spell of entropy.

At Hong Kong a group of tourists block my view from the landing stage, and rather than push through them I retreat; in Tokyo there is a monstrous fire, spreading above the ceiling limit, which entices me for an instant, but even at a distance of miles the fire brings sweat and I decide to repeat; in Paris I am caught by the aspect of a prostitute, curling herself into some intricate agonized pattern to the corner of the stage. She flicks me a glance as tender as yearning and a hand as hard as stone, and once again I ponder, then decide not, the deeper odors of Paris winding through me, and I return to the Transporter for the last time. Each jolt is terrifying; each is exhilarating. Diving in for the last time, I have the sensation of passage.

This happens after a series of trips; instancy declines as the Cage Effect begins to double; and when I emerge at Trinidad a thousand years of screaming later, it is with the realization that I can go no farther; that if I subject myself to the Transporter yet again before resting I will run deep into the full implications of the Effect – the dragons and the sense of dredging the underside of the Universe – and I am geared for nothing like that, not now.

So in Trinidad I come off the parapet, join the crowds in the streets. There is nothing remarkable in my disparity, nothing strange in my garb: Trinidad is the last city of mingling, the last city laid close to the ground, and there is nothing remarkable about my aspect or that of the naked women who stand in line on the streets, stroking their breasts and chuckling; the old man flinging tapes against the sky, screaming for redemption; the four priests Final Tripping in a subterranean corridor jutting off the street which has become their impromptu temple. Nothing remarkable about any of that; an ease to Trinidad which I have attended many times before, always to satisfaction; and my purposes, muddy at first, clarify as I push my way through the streets, ignoring the screaming of the beggars: I have come here for epiphany. Nothing less will do.

At the church of the epiphanies I check my pockets for the proper papers, then push my way through the crowds bulking at one of the side doors, screaming for a sign of grace from the chapel. There has been a time when I have been among those crowds; when I believed that the grace which would come to those unable to fit their way into the service itself would be the purest and finest of all because it would come peripheral to the spirit, a dark, gentle, sidewise angel's kiss. But that was a long time ago, and I do not believe any of this now. The church is an engine, much like the engine of the appropriated Cadillac; it must be administered to and treated often if it is to function.

In the enclosure itself there are people spread out among the pews, some of them having already received epiphany stoned out, collapsed over the pews; others, muttering intensely to themselves, have not yet made that decision, but there is no time for hesitancy now. My time is limited; I must return to the Transporter shortly, but I cannot face the mind of Cage without grace, and so I push myself to the altar and wait then until a Priest comes from the side. An idle Priest this, and as I look penetratingly at him our glances link, and then he is kneeling on the side, looking down at me. He is an old man, in his upper thirties, little splits beginning in the riven cheeks, but his hands are soft and firm as they come downward. 'Epiphany?' he says.

'Epiphany.'

'Do you have the proper credentials?'

It is required. Not long ago I understand it was still possible to receive epiphany at Trinidad anonymously, but when the suicides mounted, when more and more began to discover what had been a prized secret, that the Final Trip was available under any conditions to whatever age, there was a massive purge, and now most of the Priests are themselves agents of the various capitals. At least this is the rumor; the undisputed fact is that they work under the orders of the capitals and can function rigidly only with proper credentials. I show him the papers, he leans forward, his eyes glittering, and for one moment the obscene thought occurs to me that I could topple him, send him staggering into the box against me, where I could turn upon him the full force of my desire and scream out the questions, but some chanting of *Kyrie Eleison* from far back, a chant which reminds me of the renegade Priests in the alleyway, diverts my thoughts, and I think of this no longer. The one on the altar hands back the papers. 'That is proper,' he says. 'Everything is in order. What do you want?'

'Epiphany.'

'What matter of epiphany?'

I relish the question, turning it over in mind, thinking for an instant of all the possibilities opened to me. Sexual, psychological, spiritual, mortal, immortal, corruptive – all of these are available to me, and to consider these possibilities is to have restored to me, if only briefly, the illusion of choice which epiphany proffers. But it passes away, and as always I am rooted in the dull box of self. 'Spiritual,' I say.

'Spiritual,' the Priest says. 'That is quite agreeable.'

The Priest returns to his part of the altar, where he opens a sliding shelf and begins to forage. Watching him amidst the wafting smell of incense coming now from the blower beneath me, I wonder how long it will be until he has joined his brothers in the alleyways. What is the life of a Priest at epiphany? But it is merely an idle consideration: it means nothing; my breath becomes rapid as he returns with the censers and a tinted

34

synthetic gold headpiece. He bows, hands it to me. 'Spiritual,' he says; 'would you like a blessing?'

'A blessing is not necessary.'

'A blessing can only help and lend augmentation to your prayers.'

I look through the lines of the fallen throughout the church and then at the face of the Priest; no difference as far as I can see, no difference in any of them. All operate at the same remove from sacrament, and it would take very little, I understand, very little at all, for the Priest to be in the line of those fallen; they he, he they: all of it would be the same. It is not worth the disputation. I bow my head slowly, ironically, wondering if the irony of this will come through, and say, 'Very well then, but only a brief one, a prayer of brevity.' All prayers involve an extra token for the church.

'All prayers must be brief,' the Priest says, 'just as mercy itself must be very brief before the eternal and pending fire,' and murmurs something in one of the older tongues, words colliding against one another in ritual which I can barely distinguish; and then, removing something from my pocket, again he is gone. I tighten the headpiece into place, turn the dials.

Slowly, familiarly, remission spreads through me. It has happened this way before and will happen again; the church is one of the constancies, and slowly the headpiece drives its great splinters through the brain, impaling sensation on a spit, sensation slowly turning, illuminated under the sudden lights. Now I see Jag, his face torn and twisted in the great vault of the Final Trip, and beyond that I see the Four Priests of the alley; these, then, will be the constituents of the vision, what the mind has given back to the persona, and as that picture begins to circulate through, the colors appear and I sink deeply into it. Now Jag has joined the Four Priests; they are whispering mysteriously, conferring behind their hands, and then I see his body bob and plummet to the alley, the Final Trip overtaking him, and the Priests remove their garments and cover him. Under their garments they are naked, and as they begin to dance, their bodies take on a sensual light. I see the angles and orifices of their bodies and feel an instant of vagrant desire, the desire shifting as the bodies merge, coalesce, become a gigantic body which sprouts breasts and hair to cover the pubis, which becomes, as I regard, a vagina; and then the body is that of Sherry, and in the epiphany I plunge into her repeatedly, finding

35

her as thick and moist now as ever I did in the spaces of the car in the coupling room.

It is gasping and exceedingly painful, but it is also all that has been promised, even to the chants of Latin which overtake the background as I plunge with Sherry to mate in the room of the mind, and I give myself wholly over to it, shaking, shuddering, feeling that indeed I am on the verge of something profound, but as I reach forward to touch it, Jag suddenly reappears, distended to gigantic height, and into one bare arm he repeatedly shoves, over and again, the needle of the Final Trip in reciprocity to my own jabbing movements until they become intertwined. Oh my, I gasp, falling down the tube of self, and there is a long, flat space in which I perceive nothing at all; when I come out of this –

– I am in the streets of Trinidad once again, winds coming through me, crowds around, sounds like great birds in the air; and a small man is beating, beating, beating at the doors of the whorehouse which I pass, and, epiphany or none, it is time to reenter the Transporter, the machine that will send hunks of me back to Dance Complex . . . and no closer to epiphany than ever before.

In nights which follow I dream of the Priest who served me.

VI

Standing on the high parapet, looking at the layers of the city knifed through rubble, tall gleaming sections of Dance thrown against ruins I will never understand, I think of Jag once more through the light of epiphany and feel for one instant that I have grasped everything in simultaneity. Past and present, even little stark glimpses of the future congeal through the haze, perceptible even through the filtered glass . . . but the moment passes; it has been induced in any event by palliatives, cannot be taken seriously. And I turn to see S. L. Combest (1974–1999) standing beside me on the parapet in a posture of gloom, wearing his familiar period costume. Another of my celebrated dead, but more contentious than any of them. Beads glisten against his bare chest; his movements take on light. I can see that it is going to be difficult now.

'Listen,' S.L. says in his high, sweet revolutionary's voice, 'you have got to change all of this.'

'Come now,' I say. Sometimes a reasonable attitude is best, meeting his illogic with banter rather than spite. 'It's immutable. Nothing can be changed.'

'You've got to try.'

'Everyone tries. I'm doing the best I can, surely.'

'No,' S.L. says. Humor is not his meat today; he will be ingenuous and blunt. 'I mean it, I really do,' and as before, I receive some impression of the power that he must have had to move crowds so very long ago. 'It's not enough to talk of private solutions, private flight – '

'You mean the Final Trip,' I say. With S.L. it is necessary to force the point or hang like a pendulum in the clock of dialectic forever. 'That's what you mean.'

'Of course it's what I mean. This Final Trip you keep on dealing with isn't a means of coping with it at all.'

'I think it's a goddamned good means of coping. I don't want to argue with you, but I think it's a great means.'

'Society says that it's against the Final Trip,' S.L. says, not listening, which is his habit. 'That's the word that comes out of the capital. How they want to do everything they can to discourage it. But that's all a bunch of shit; you know that. They love it, they depend on it, they make it illicit and attractive.'

'It's damned attractive.'

'Generation after generation, it's the best people, the people who could have exerted the force to change, who are taking it, because they think it's the only viable protest. Society loves that; that's just what they want. Don't you understand?' S.L. says.

'Yes, I understand. Do *you* understand? You're talking about a world you've never seen, a world you don't know; Transporters and complexes are the way we live now, and in Groups. Do you know what those are?'

For a moment S.L. seems confused; his eyes mist over. 'No,' he says. 'No, I don't. But it doesn't make any difference. The human condition is always the same; the nature of the beast is always unchanging.'

'Bullshit,' I say to this phantom. 'Everything has changed. We are aliens to you.'

'No, you are not. Nothing human is alien. Life, wherever it

is lived – how can it be alien? Anyway,' S.L. says vaguely, looking out at the complex, 'let's get back to the subject. Let's not get diverted; don't miss the point.' He points downward. 'There is where your battle lies. There is where you must make the changes.'

'Crap.'

'*That's* the Final Trip,' he says, waving an arm awkwardly. The gesture almost unbalances him. For one disastrous instant I fear that S.L. might fall. All indications are that Combest has a certain physical clumsiness and lack of grace which as much as anything else contributed to his spectacular death. Of course I am not clear about any of these details; it is not a subject of interest, and I specifically exclude revolutionary history from my topics of research. This has nothing to do with the phantoms who choose to visit, however: I am tone-deaf, but this did not keep Beethoven away.

All I can see here are the clumsiness and the rhetorical power, that ability to sway crowds which I can comprehend because in his fashion Combest can even sway *me*, even though I know he is not real. None of them are real, but that doesn't make it any easier for me. Of course twenty-five in those times was not a ripe age to die (although I would consider S.L. quite elderly), and had he lived longer he might have effected greater changes, but as it was he effected nothing at all. He seems to know this himself; it explains his restlessness, his inability to give up an argument even when he knows he is hopelessly without facts to support it.

'The hell with it,' I say, not knowing if I am addressing the image beside me or merely talking to the complex itself and the ruined city over which it stands. 'It just doesn't matter,' and I turn then from the parapet, eager to get inside, afraid of the sickening temptation I have felt to hurl myself over the edge; even though the saving screens would block me, I would still have too much to explain. 'None of this matters at all,' but as I try to go inside, Combest is still there, waving his arms, blocking my path forcibly.

'You cannot walk from this so easily,' he says. 'Damn it, you cannot desert the sense and substance of your life.' His eyes assume a purer light; in fact he might be having an epiphany of his own. 'Consider the changes to be made,' he says hoarsely.

'The period of change is gone.'

'It is merely beginning! When you think that change cannot be accomplished, it means that everything is at the period of revolution.'

'Crap,' I say again. It is wearying. I walk into my cubicle; S.L. pursues. 'The society is delicately poised on chaos and madness; it is insupportable; it is so dependent upon the machines and the Final Trip as the means of getting rid of the revolutionaries that one interception of the machinery at the right time and place would make all of it come to a stop.'

'Wrong era,' I say, running a hand against the wall. 'There are no chaos and madness here. There's hardly any machinery, either; not that I know of. Just the Transporter. But that's not a machine; it's a miracle. And the Final Trip is just great. I'm all for it.'

S.L. still will not listen. He reclines against a wall, drops to a knee in a dramatic posture. 'There comes a time,' he says, 'a time when the machine is so brutal, so ignorant of human desires that it must be stopped.'

'Oh yes?'

'Bring it to a halt; slam a human hand right into its entrails and make it stop.'

'That's Savio,' I point out; 'you probably got all of that from him, but of course it didn't come to much,' and push my way roughly and abruptly past him, kick out a foot. S.L., surprised, falls drearily on his nose with a squeak and begins to pick himself up on all fours as I move into the cubicle proper, looking at the gray assemblage of tapes and recoveries lining the mattress, eye the gray stains of semen which have the aspect of teardrops on the dull sheets. I simply cannot control myself even with full access to Sherry; masturbation is a phenomenon so powerful that it contains its own satisfactions. Waste, however, waste: there must be something better to do with it, something better to do with all the pieces of my life. But what? Only the Final Trip looks attractive, and I am not quite ready for that, not just yet. I want to see how Jagway takes it before I make that gesture.

'Go away,' I say. S.L. has crouched to a half-posture and is still talking, pursuing me. 'I've said everything there is to say. I do not wish to continue this. There is nothing to discuss, and I'd appreciate your going.' Can you unbid the celebrated dead?

'Nineteen hundred and ninety-nine,' Combest says. 'That was two years before 2001, just months until the millennium.

I gave my life, my very *life*, so that you could be free and make the choices, so that you could tear the cities from their roots and become men again, and what have we?'

'Beats me. Beats me what we have. Why don't you get the hell out of here?'

'We have a nightmare age.'

'Not from the inside.'

'The obscenity of Final Trips, Survival Groups, weeds growing over the highways, while the poisons still run free – '

'Is that a fact . . . ' I say. 'Is that a goddamned fact,' and then patience lurches; I do not know how much of S.L. is real and how much unconscious projection; how much of what he is saying comes from outside and how much I have created myself. But whatever the origin, I am no longer interested, have no interest whatsoever in his accusations, and so, deserting all bravura calm which I have cultivated in my relationships with the celebrated dead, even with (up until now) Combest, I say, 'Get out! Get out of my room, get out of my complex, get out of my life!' moving then to strike with a gnarled fist, hitting him in his insubstantial head and chest, and I feel flesh, not dreams, before me, his flesh porous, neither ghostly nor insubstantial but real in the room, as real as Sherry's. His eyes pulp out; my fingers weave through the gelatin of his flesh.

'You can't beat me,' he says, his voice coming out with droplets of blood from the corners of his mouth, which I find enormously satisfying. 'You can't avoid your problems by beating me, Sid; oh, Sid, you've got to face them, face up to them; the situation can no longer be avoided.'

I hit him in the throat. He groans and whines. 'Tell me again,' I say. 'Tell me what I can't avoid. *Tell me.*'

And, damaged, he nevertheless talks: inexhaustibly talking. 'You're living this,' he says. 'I'm dreaming but you are *living*; this is your life; no construction, but a world and a life; your life the only future that most of us can ever know,' and the truth of this, the sheer, damaging authority with which the cringing old revolutionary says this, drives me quite over that lip of insanity on which I have been dancing since these visits began.

I reach forward to hurl him into the hall, then kick him into bloodspots, send him out of my life . . . but instead I overbalance. My feet slip from underneath. For a perilous instant I hang suspended like a sheet, weaving before S.L., and then slowly, slowly, toppling in little stages, I collapse before him, and then, in transmutation, it is he rather than I who controls the situation. His eyes regard me through their moisture in a kind of stricken and honest gloom; his face crooks into a smile; smells of the charnel house drift from the hall into my abused nostrils; and then, not surprisingly, he is gone. I do not see him anymore, only the sound of his recollected screams filling the hall as I stand there.

Oh, Combest, S.L. Combest (1974–1999), why could it not have been fifty years later that it happened to you in your bed so that, informed with restlessness, you would not be stalking through these spaces and making my life, or at least my portion of life, the only slice of it I will ever know, completely untenable?

I have a tendency, now and then, to snivel a bit, but this is part of my personality.

VII

I decide that I must confer with Jag, discuss his F.T. with him, find out how he is taking the decision, how it sits with him, what his plans are up until the point that he actually does it, and in fact am almost on the point of going to his cubicle to bring up the issue, searching information, but before I do this, Jag himself intercepts me in a wasteway and pursues me all the way to the Transfer Point, talking unbidden about his views and experiences. His personality seems to have changed, now that he has made the decision. Once talkative, always possessed with himself and his reactions; but now he has become compulsive about his reminiscences, imparting that sense of horrid confidentiality which all of us in the Group have learned to be suspicious about . . . but he is quite beyond the Group now.

And although I was initially curious, I find, listening, that it is quite difficult to put up with him, although I tell myself that I must. After all, it is not his fault that he now wishes to talk; the F.T. is a very large decision for any of us to make, and he is not to be blamed for wanting to talk about that compulsively. Also, the chief teaching of the Group, if any teaching can be said to be devised from our engagements, is that we must bear tolerance for one another; we must have respect for all of our individual desires in or out of this world, because the alternative, the alternative to tolerance, would be unthinkable. We would certainly turn aggressive and sullen. So we must, if at all possible, avoid violent confrontation. We must learn to get along. We must also learn to go along.

'So when are you going to do it?' I say, cutting off a stream of jargon about his sexual responses to Claire, pivoting, holding him against a wall. 'Tell me, what have you decided?'

His eyes narrow, show a little cunning. Duplicity was never something I would associate with Jag; many changes have been made. The anticipation of death will always induce a double-level. 'I'm not sure yet,' he says.

'Not sure?'

'I have decided not to do it today,' he says, putting a hand on me, stroking delicately, his fingertips patting up to the ulna, 'and I do think that I will avoid tomorrow as well. This is not to say that I won't be doing it soon.'

'Yes, of course.'

'I'm always ready to do anything soon, and I've made the decision, but not for the moment. It's too interesting knowing that I'm going to die, that I can get out of this anytime I want. In fact, it's almost bearable.'

'I know what you mean.'

'I'll wait until I feel like doing it. It won't be more than a few more shifts, though. The important thing is that the event has been decided.' He winks at me. 'When are you going to do it?' he says. 'It's all a pack of shit, you know.'

'Oh, I know.'

'So when?'

'I'm thinking about it,' I say. 'When I'm ready to, I will.'

'You're taking that little whore, Sherry, aren't you?'

'Sometimes,' I say.

'I thought so. You're stealing cars out of the armory, going out into the hills and putting it to her. Slicing it right in.' He licks his lips, rubs against the wall, his mouth salivating. His eyes are a little wild. 'I knew it all the time,' he says. 'You can't keep anything from me. Not the way we live here.'

'I didn't try to.'

'I know what's going on. I know what's going on with everyone. How is it? Tell me what it's like; I want to know.'

I look at him, into the pools of his eyes, and decide that although he is sympathetic and his decision is a sensible one, he is probably crazy. This does not reduce the efficacy of the Final Trip, but it leads to a question which I know I will have to consider later: does one have to be insane to do it? Or is it a sign of heroism and health? Abruptly I feel that I must leave him, but he makes a detaining gesture; I feel the metallic contact of his fingers, coming against my sleeve. 'Tell me,' he says, 'tell me what it's like. I want to know. I deserve to know. Come on; I'll tell you everything about Claire.'

'Nothing,' I say, trying to shrug off the pincers of his insect-grip. 'I will say absolutely nothing about that.'

'You can tell me, old friend.'

'I don't want to tell you. I don't want to tell anyone.'

'Tell Jag, old friend,' he says hoarsely. 'I'm going out of the way soon. Think how it will be when you remember me and that you never gave old Jag one of his last wishes. Aren't you putting it to her? I mean, I know you are, but I want to hear you say it.'

'It doesn't matter,' I say. 'It just doesn't matter, damn it,' opening up a little ground in front of him, moving with grace and desire. It is only a few yards, after all, to the Transfer Point, and I encourage myself with little moans and mumbles – *Sid oh you Sid you can do it you can do it Sid oh kid* – and the Transporter will flip me through then to Peking, where I will take Oriental gymnastics before stopping off in Tokyo for a quick look at Hiroshima, with which I perpetually renew myself now and again, then back to Dance for what I conceive of to be a difficult meeting with Sherry – but he holds me by the clothing, holds me tightly, eases me into a wall. I can feel little spots of damp gathering at the place where he is touching me.

'What does it feel like?' Jag says and winks. 'It's not for me, that kind of stuff, but I want to know. Is it good?'

Reticence and fear mingle. He has become stronger than I through his decision; I can no longer deny this. 'It's all right,' I say. 'There are worse things. Worse things to do.'

'Do you come?'

'Sometimes.'

'Does she help you come?'

'Sometimes,' I say, 'and sometimes not.' He is really mad. 'I have to go to Hong Kong,' I say.

'Always going somewhere, you Sid. Always on the move. Don't you ever stay still, Sid? Stay still and think of the F.T.'

43

'Let me go,' I say, bringing a hand up like a lever, breaking his grip, disentangling. 'Let me go now.'

He backs off, then leaps as if dodging imaginary pellets being flung by some demented hand in the latticework of the Transporter. 'I knew it,' he says. 'I knew all the time it had to be that way. Had to!' His hands smooth little folds on his cheeks. 'Is it worth it?'

'I must go.'

'I'm going to Trip soon. You have to tell me everything I want to know. That's the way it is; you know that, Sid. Is it worth it? That's all I want to know; that's what I want to hear from you. I've been thinking of getting into that kind of stuff myself before I F.T.'

'You've had it.'

'No I haven't. Claire and I just play, never anything more. Didn't you know that, Sid? I thought you knew it. We don't do much of anything at all. Should I bother penetrating?'

'How can I tell you?' I say, barely able to absorb this new information. 'How can I tell you what to do? You've got to make the choices yourself.'

'I have.'

'Then make this one,' I say. 'I cannot help you. No one can help you now.'

And this much is true; I have passed truth on in the exchange. Inside, I find myself flaming with the sudden urge to tell Jag of my own condition; to tell him that I am constantly assaulted by the famous dead; that the famous dead come into my room during sleep and even at isolated periods of waking now to confer with me, to advise, admonish, elucidate, lecture; that I am unable to disentangle myself from these dead. Barely able to deal with the living, I am now in a network of the dead and almost nowhere to turn, no one with whom I can share this pressing and very real set of problems. But I hold back. I tell him nothing. Jag is really crazy; his decision has purified him, washed away the extraneous parts of his personality which held the madness in check, so that now he is aflame with it. Jag would be the last with whom to share my many recent difficulties. He must see this; at some level there is a rapid exchange of information, eye to eye; but the moment goes away and he holds back from inquiry. There is more working within us than we can ever express.

'I've made this decision,' Jag says, backing away, and I walk to the Transporter; then, holding back with strange reluctance, pause and turn toward him. The wasteway is deserted, the Transporter clean and beckoning, but I cannot somehow leave him. 'I *have* made it – you know it's the truth, Sid – but I can't seem to follow through.'

'It's your decision,' I say. 'You can do whatever you wish.'

'I *have* made it. The only problem is that something is holding me back. It's one thing to make a decision, but it's quite another to go ahead and *do* it, if you follow what I mean; this just isn't so easy for me. It isn't easy at all.'

'It isn't easy for any of us.'

'But if you decided to F.T., wouldn't you just go ahead and *do* it?' Jag says despairingly, but I have placed myself against the wall. Using the planes of my back, then, like clever sucking little tentacles to draw me nearer the chute, my body has made the decision: I am going to leave him. All of the time that I thought I was focusing attention I was really moving toward that chute, and now at last I am on top of it.

Too late, Jag sees me. 'You can't do this,' he says. 'You can't leave me!'

'I've got to. I have no choice.'

'You've got to stay and talk to me,' he says as I draw myself into the wires' embrace and focus the leads. 'You can't just go away. You've got to help me understand why I'm not ready to do it.'

But it is too late. The generators tug at me. I feel intimations of power, pull my identification kit from the hidden corner pocket and shove it into the feeder line for verification, then light is all around me, and I am being fed into the shuttle like yards of rope. Only my intelligence is left, pure intelligence hanging in the air, the last part of me as always to be devoured by the Transporter, and it is this intelligence that encircles Jag as I depart. It seems that he is cursing for having been abandoned. His curses are pure slivers that drive through me like nails as, deep in the heart of the Transporter, I slide down the line of the Hong Kong shuttle, all of me then for the moment merely energy, pure energy colliding with that vanished city.

VIII

In Historicity and Cultural Devising we are asked to consider the Kennedy Car. It was a late-model bulletproof limousine of a type we can still see in the grand Tokyo exhibit, shielded from atmosphere by layers of lead, absolutely impenetrable . . . and yet on the day that Kennedy was killed, this marvelous car that surrounded him on all levels with protection was open instead to the elements; the roof was down, providing the assassin with a clear shot. This proves, the tapes says, the absolute perversity of our forebears: on the one hand they would devise an optimum protective device, and on the other they would then fail out that device in a way that would make it useless. Does this show the ambivalence of the ancients in their relationship to life and death: the simultaneous courting and avoidance of disaster as a reflection of their own unclear state of decision on mortality? Was the parading of leaders through the streets open to the hands of assassins a form of the ritual sacrifice, a technological elaboration of what had been a much older code, that every now and then leaders had to be destroyed by the populace in order to revive and renew? Was it true that by the codes of ritual sacrifice the leader himself embodied, took unto himself all the evil of the nation, and therefore his removal was a healthy purgation?

These are questions worth considering, and the tapes beckon us to consider, but the object at issue is the car itself. Eight cylinders, five hundred cubic inches, overhead valve, full power system, sliding panels and gauged roof, a car in which a leader could sit like a king, gnarled but protected from even the most vagrant of breezes from the outside, a car that had been constructed to be impenetrable . . . and yet, flung open, became the conveyance of death. Speculation falls aside; philosophical considerations mean nothing; everything comes down to the matter of the car. Perhaps by understanding it we can understand the essential mysteries. So we go over the car in schematic, inch by inch, examining the stress of the metal, the framing of the joints, the workings of the internal combustion engine, looking for knowledge like jelly to be squeezed out of those spaces, and somewhere during the middle of this I have an insight, a unique and powerful insight: it explains my fascination with the old Cadillac and why I am so magnificently potent only within its confines. There is nothing illegal about fornication in the complex; it is, as a matter of fact, encouraged. Nevertheless, I am only able to function within the car. This is highly interesting – in fact it may be central – and I advise myself to give this more consideration. Did the agents, I wonder, create the Final Trip, or did they merely pass it down as an idea to succeeding generations who would be more able to perceive its beauty and implications than those agents of the past who could not even decide whether they wanted to kill the King or merely preserve him?

IX

Out among the weeds of 1-80, the car ticking to silence once again, I impale myself upon Sherry, slowly wind myself into her, whispering encouragements and secrets into her ear. Our couplings have become ritualized, not acknowledged by either of us during shift except by small glances and squeezings of the hand, but they are resumed compulsively at night over and over again, three or four times a week now, sometimes more if I can arrange other commitments, keep her warm and persuaded.

There is serious valve trouble in the Cadillac. Despite all of my attempts to bring the device into alignment, sooner or later compression failure beckons; hopefully not while we are on the road, where we would have to stay, embarrassingly, until help came through one of the rare patrols that grace this section. These couplings have elements of danger.

I cannot, cannot be concerned by the future anyway, not while we are on the road and I have all I can do to manage within the transparent frame of the present. Penetrating her deeply then to the last inch, I begin to move up and down upon her, expostulating, then comforting, silence all around, the rich metallic odors of the car filling my nostrils, overwhelming the frail scent which comes from Sherry herself. How familiar these motions! – the constancy is a comfort. In that posture I see little absent flickers of light, see those vanished buildings in the weeds, imagine that I can hear the sounds of the city, the junkyard of technology richly slamming through its processes, those sounds overcoming the peeps and admonitions which issue from Sherry's mouth. Copulation is a reinforcement of

47

the identity which even the F.T. cannot wholly embrace.

And there is a moment in which I think I am achieving full perception, a moment during which I feel that I am about to learn something that has never occurred to me before, that will completely change my life . . . but as that insight seizes me by the scruff of the neck, dragging me from her, it is only a familiar moment, the easy cheat of sex which quickly passes, and I come out of the other end of her diminished, liquefied, all of me weakened, and know then that the moment has passed. There has never been any constancy in our joining, or in my joining with anyone; I have been doing it since I was eight, and it is always the same. Nothing is changed. One must slither from the depths like a fish and rejoin the poisonous light of the world.

She pats her hair, brings herself into place as I collapse crosswise, ballooning in depression over her. I am too depressed to talk, and a sob comes from me which I choke down: I will not show emotion. Always she must believe that I am the stronger.

'What do you want, Sid?' she says. 'Tell me, what do you want?'

'I don't know.'

'You must.'

'But I don't,' I say, rearing from her, pressing my shoulders into the slick leather of the car. I simply do not know. High above me, on a parapet, I dream that the assassin is watching me, tracking with his rifle. Soon he will level . . . even to the swamps, and where will I be then? 'I don't know,' I say again. 'I want nothing.'

Shockingly she says, 'Do you want to Final Trip? Is that what you're thinking about?'

'How can you say something like that?' Now I come off the seat as if indeed the bullet had blown home, my joints feeling metallic. 'How can you say that – '

'I was just asking,' she says. Her voice quivers, and I can tell that she is really terrified. 'Just asking now; you don't have to get mad at me. I only thought you might want it. I don't know. I've been thinking about it myself. I mean, Jag thought – '
And then she stops, distracted, pats her hair once again.

Zooming closer in some quick-lens facet, timestop, I can see Sherry as she will look in twenty years if she lives – make it ten – her face a caved-in artifact of this night, the little sensors

48

of her eyes peering from the quick rubble, conveying messages. She could be frozen and convey to researchers all of the twenty-third century. 'Sid,' she says, 'Sid, don't just stay there, don't – '

'I don't want to Final Trip,' I say, and in the speaking know that this is so; many of my moods are subterranean; they must be given words before I know what is truly on my mind. In this respect, I am very much like a machine. 'The Final Trip is the poor way out, the assassin's route.'

'Is it?'

'Yes, it is; it is a means of escape. It has nothing to do with life as it is lived, and that is what we must understand, that *these* are our one and only lives.'

It comes to me that I have been following nothing less than the advisements of S.L. Combest. Not only are my dead assaulting me in the open spaces of my cubicle; I am carrying them around in the packing case of the skull, and this is quite infuriating. I can feel the bile beginning to work within. Sherry looks at me with concern. 'You dirty little whore,' I say. 'You dirty little whore.' Not a pleasant confidence, but that is the way I feel; it has come out of me that strongly, that strangely, that I lunge against her, crack her cheek with the back of my hand. 'I don't have to take this anymore,' I say. 'Do you understand that? I don't have to!'

She rears in the car; her head collides into the plastic of the window and then rebounds, comes toward me in tears and grimace. 'Stop it!' she says. 'Stop it now! I add my voice to this: Sid, I tell myself, *stop it, Sid, stop it, you fool, she has nothing to do with this at all, it is not her fault, none of it is connected to her but has to do only with you, even Combest* – and at last this works; the urge to strike comes from me slowly, oozing out in drips and drops. I look at her, she looks at me, and something in that exchange of glances tells me that it is all over between the two of us and that we will not be going out on this road again . . . but underneath, there is another understanding, which is that this is all illusion compounded from my guilt and she barely exists, barely exists; I can do anything I want with her so long as I care; she can hardly be called an independent object.

What is it? Which is correct? Does it matter? The concepts collide, intertwine, and I put my hands on the wheel, shaking, trying to conceal from her how truly distraught I am now. It occurs to me that I am indeed very ill, as ill as hell, so to speak, that there is a sickness of a kind I have never before acknowledged, and that something has happened not only to the mind but to the heart, and that I am not the person I took myself to be, that all along I made judgments as if I were one kind, and all this time I was another.

I start the motor, hearing the thump of ignition, the dead whir of fan blades, and for a second I think it will not catch, but then it does reluctantly, wiring almost blowing apart under the strain. I ease the steering to the left, play the accelerator, slide the car, sucking, out of the mud. Against the door, Sherry sits crumpled, a mass of laundry, that is all, looking at me from those introspective, shielded eyes, and I wonder how I could ever have found her so attractive, how I could have allowed this snaffling, sniveling lust to overtake me, when all along there were more important things to consider. But she will say nothing in reply; she has no messages to impart. Terror has compressed her to silence.

'I meant what I said, you know,' I point out, driving. 'I don't think the Final Trip is right.'

She shakes her head and says, 'I don't even want to talk about it.'

'But I shouldn't have done what I did.'

'You can do anything you want. It doesn't matter to me.'

'I'm upset,' I say. 'Jag has got me all fucked up. I don't know how to deal with it – don't you see that? I just don't know what to do anymore.'

'You won't find out from me,' she says. 'Sid, I am not going to tell you that.'

And so now we go back on the stones of I-80, Sherry moving closer, touching me with a hip. We are near one another, still friends; and yet the connection is insubstantial. In some real sense it does not exist at all; just as the old songs have always advised, we are in different worlds. But the depths of the pain which has been brought by my realization that I do not and therefore cannot F.T. . . . it is not something I find easy to accept.

S.L. was right, however. The Final Trip must be a deceit. For if it were not, would Jag be so unhappy?

I know that this will be the last time, the very last between us in this way, or at least I hope it will be the last between: there is no way that I can continue to be with a human who

50

now knows the shameful fact: that I do not have the courage to accept the goal we must all cherish.

No knowledge, no desire; merely pain, and the car crashing the night.

X

Hugh Cage (1968–2023), the nominal inventor of the Transporter and for sure the holder of all the patents, greets me enthusiastically upon my return. 'How are you doing?' he says. He is an ebullient man; all of the tapes point this out again and again. Although blessed with scientific genius, he never thought of himself as being a serious researcher or making a serious contribution. Actually, all that he wanted to do, say the tapes, was to 'open up the world' to people, to 'give them fun'. For all these reasons he should be perfectly good company, but I have had enough, quite enough, of my celebrated dead by this time, and wish that he would go. Hugh Cage, however, can hardly take a hint, and there is no way to eject him forcibly from quarters . . . so instead, while he babbles on to me, I do something that is quite rare; go to supply and take three mediums. Only during circumstances of the greatest strain would I ever consider indulging in mediums . . . but I do not see how, at this time, I can do otherwise. Meanwhile Cage prates on; he has been checking out the Transporters in the corridors; most of them are in good condition, but the access switches on several are not functioning properly. 'Disgraceful!' he booms. 'And it's such an easy thing to maintain properly. Of course I'm glad to see that it's so popular.'

'Oh yes,' I say, 'oh yes indeed, it's very popular.'

'Every level has one – is that right?'

'Every level. They're cheap and easy to duplicate, so this was what they decided to do.'

'A wonderful idea,' Cage says and then squints, walks to a high point near the parapet, looks down through the opaque glass. 'Just tell me one thing, son, what's that peculiar smell?'

'Smell? I don't notice any smell. Would you mind very much leaving?'

'You're not conscious of that, son? It must be ozone or something like that. Things seem to have pretty well deteriorated from my day, let me tell you that. They sure have – '

'Everything deteriorates,' I say. 'That is the factor of entropy.' The mediums are beginning to take hold. I feel myself sliding along a tube that leads to a lighted place at the end; momentarily much seems without consequence, which, of course, is the purpose of mediums. Neither good nor bad, neither disaster nor destiny awaits us; what we are doing is simply getting along. Much of everything does not matter; that is the message which the mediums pass along the circuits of the blood, and they suit me now. 'Hey,' I say, 'I really would appreciate it if you'd leave. Things have been very difficult for me recently, and it's not easy to put up constantly – '

'Oh, don't be ridiculous, son,' Cage says. He perches on the floor, a neatly assembled little man, birdlike in his features, birdlike in his hands, the floor seemingly a nest underneath him. 'If you could do anything about this, you know that you certainly would, but inasmuch as you can't, we're both condemned to getting along as best we can. What seems to be your problem, anyway? Stuff yourself into one of my machines and get out of your world.'

'I have,' I say. 'Everybody goes everywhere. But still there are problems.'

'Really?' Cage says. 'It's hard enough to deal with one thing before getting involved with the next. Actually, I'm still trying to deal with the fact of my own death, you know. It was a stunning surprise. I was in the best of health and I was making plans twenty years ahead.'

'Nowadays you don't have to do that. Make plans twenty years ahead.'

'Oh, plans are always good,' Cage says. Confusion, like an animal, scuttles across the planes of his face. 'At least I've been led to think so. Hard to tell.'

There is a slight pause during which I realize that Cage is waiting for me to say something. Like all ebullient men, he can hold up his part of the conversation only to a certain point; then he is desperately in need of encouragement. Since there is no way in which I can get rid of him, there is the real chance that he will merely sit in this posture until dawn, his ebullience at last converted to sobs. To be polite, then, I say, 'Tell me, how did you get around to inventing it?'

'Inventing it? Inventing what? Oh, the Transporter. Well, I just thought that a cheap, clean, easy device that would open the world to the common man, instantaneous transit, would solve a lot of problems and also be quite interesting.'

'Yes, it is.'

'There was a good deal of international tension in my time. It seemed to me that it was created by the compartmentalization of souls, whereas if people had instant access to all parts of the world, they would tend to think of themselves as world citizens, or at least would no longer regard others as foreigners. And what with the abandonment of space travel, it didn't look as if there were going to be too many open places out there for a while, so we might as well make the whole Earth open. Wasn't that a good idea?'

'It was a wonderful idea,' I say; 'it even works.'

'Well of course it works. I notice that things are pretty much the same, though; people still live in one place.'

'More or less,' I say. 'Is there any way I can persuade you to leave?'

'Oh my dear boy,' Cage says with a giggle, 'oh my dear, unfortunate boy, that's an impossible question, don't you know that? Of course you can get me to leave anytime you want. You've conjured me up; you can make me go.'

'Go, then.'

'You don't really want me to. If you did I'd vanish, you know. But I'm afraid that at some level you want my presence here.' He shrugs elaborately. 'Don't blame me; it's not my fault after all.'

And looking at him, seeing Cage in the sudden angled shadows of light, I see that what he is saying is right and that I cannot dispute him: his body is translucent, the squares of the floor visible through it; he exists here on my sufferance, conjured up merely because I want him; and the reasons for this, the reasons for my wanting him, that is, are so obscure that I will be unable to deduce them. They are lost to me like everything else. Fixed, his smile has the wrenched, strained aspect of a man in severe pain. In this still-life I can see the web of cracks around his eyes, the faint corruption stirring in his forehead, which indicates, as no testimony ever could, that Cage must have been a very sick man toward the end, that his death was not unexpected at all but merely a comma to the great, continuing sweep of his life, or so he envisaged. It is sickening, considering that Cage might have fought against his death as long and hard as he could, whereas now the Final Trip is taken

53

for granted as a dignified period or at least as a semicolon to existence, less of a mystery than induction into the spaces of the Transporter. 'Remission,' I say to him. 'I want remission.'

'We all do, my lad.'

'I want it, though; I need it. I deserve remission; I can no longer go on –'

'Please,' Cage says defensively, raising his hands, 'I cannot stand emotional displays of this sort. I find them quite sickening and always futile. Please do your weeping somewhere else.'

'I'm not weeping,' I say, 'I'm not weeping,' and stumble to the mirror in the bathroom to find, of course, that I am. The knowledge is only incidental; my physical aspect no longer concerns me. 'You shouldn't have done it,' I say, coming out, going back to Cage. 'You shouldn't have made it work. You never should have been born.'

'Why do you say that?'

'If it hadn't existed, none of this would have happened,' I say. 'Don't you realize that?'

'I realize nothing.'

'You gave us the world and taught us that all of it was the same. You took even our dreams away from us. Nothing is different. Everything has become exactly alike.'

'That isn't my fault. We are talking about technology now, not ethos. If everything became the same, that's beyond my province. After all,' Cage says, 'I was only the inventor. The finger on the trigger is not responsible. It is only, always, the mind.'

'You lied to us!' I say. 'You lied to us about everything. You said that we could have the world, and all you gave back to us was ourselves!' and I launch myself upon him, another figure to be attacked; all my dialogues with the celebrated dead seem to end in this way; there does not seem to be any fashion by which I can establish an amicable relationship with them, everything leads to threats, and Cage himself seems astonished by the force of my attack, makes a rending gesture, lifts his palms to his face. 'This is ridiculous,' he says. 'I'm an old sick man. I don't see why you should be acting this way, Sid; it's your problem, not mine.' But he is terrified, I know he is; all of them sooner or later are terrified by me because I am longer and stronger than any of them; they know this, and Cage becomes paler and paler in the room, begins to turn translucent, and passes from translucence to dead whiteness; then he is gliding away, as insubstantial as the wind – more the pity, of course, that I do not have the satisfaction of beating him.

But he is gone, he is gone; only his damned Transporter remains. Cage (1968–2023) is gone and the room empty as if he had never been there. Under the harshness of the light, alone now, I feel myself ill at ease, as if I were under surveillance from the cameras hidden within the walls (their only purpose to ascertain whether someone has Final Tripped out, but you never know with these things; you simply never know what further mischief might be possible), and I must leave; only back for an instant, I nevertheless must leave as quickly as possible, and I do so then, darting awkwardly from the curtains and into the chute.

There is the feeling, as always, that something quite profound has occurred, that the dialogue with Cage is meaningful not only on its own terms but as a projection of meaning for other circumstances which will have to be investigated, but this is merely hysteria working the worn grooves of the mind, and I pay it no credence. I do not take it seriously. I have more immediate problems. I must stop Jag from taking the Final Trip.

XI

So I go to his cubicle and find that he is in Istanbul, according to his checking form; hurriedly I traverse to Istanbul, where a group of shouting Arabs pull me off the platform and hurl me into their midst, spitting curses and making demands for money; I give them some notes and make known to them that I am looking for Jag. They laugh and make signs at one another, but one of them pulls me into a little compartment underneath the stage and says that he has seen exactly the person who meets my description; he came and exited only minutes ago for another destination. Would I like to get a look at his card from the dispatch? I say that I would and the native's face turns careful; he says that it will cost me much money, perhaps more that I have on hand, and I think for a moment of abandoning this quest, because there is no need to talk to Jag now; he will return; there will be another time when I will be able to discuss this with him, but then amidst the screams of birds in their cages in the marketplace a hundred yards down it occurs to me that Jag has declared his intention to do the deed at any time, and he might do it tonight, might be doing it at this moment, plunging the knife into himself or working out the mediums, and then I cannot afford in this blaze of dedication to let him get away from me. 'All right,' I say, digging into my pockets for more notes, 'all right, whatever you ask,' and the native laughs, a clear, bright, tinkling Turkish laugh, and escorts me back to the group, who look at me with vast interest as I thrust banknotes into the short native's hands; then he smiles again, makes a gesture of delay and disappears under the platform. I hear the laughter of the others and think for an instant that I have been made a fool of, defrauded in Istanbul. This native will vanish into the Transporter himself and I will never see him again, but no, he returns, holding within a long sheet of paper which he slowly unfurls, the paper seeming to spring out of his gut. 'Ah,' he says, 'here,' and passes on a notation to me. 'This would be his slip. We keep very comprehensive records here. He went to 108 of the Brooklyn subscript.'

'Brooklyn?' I say. 'What the hell is Jag doing in Brooklyn?' but the question is so foolish that it does not even deserve acknowledgment, let alone answer. I spring toward the platform then, inflamed with urgency. It is one thing to pursue Jag like this, but quite another to pursue him to Brooklyn. I begin to grope for the combinations.

The native is standing below, looking up at me, his aspect one of sanctity. In beard and bells, he is sharply reminiscent of some biblical conception. He shakes his head, cries up to me above the noises of the crowd. 'This is no good,' he says.

'What is no good?'

'This,' he says, gesturing to the Transporter. 'This is a terrible invention.'

'True,' I say, 'true.' What else is there to point out? I could discuss my interview with Cage, but that would hardly make much sense to him. 'All true,' forcing myself into the feeder; there is a moment in which I seem to hang; the wait extends to seconds, and I wonder if what is going to happen sometime to someone is now happening to *me,* the Transporter has broken down . . . but one must have more faith in technology

56

than that; there is the familiar, spinning feeling, the implosion as the body collapses upon itself, and then Istanbul is sliding away from me in pastels and I am nowhere, everywhere, landing in an instant on the 108 stage in Brooklyn, and as I come down, amazingly, I see Jag himself to the side of the stage, standing there, looking with dull fascination at the figures coming out of the chute. I have done this many times myself: sometimes, when there is nothing else to do, it is interesting to see who is passing through; to see the variety of humanity as it courses through the arteries of the Transporter . . . but as he sees me his body bows into flight, his mouth curves to a shriek, and he is already in flight, moving at desperate speed.

I leap off the platform in pursuit, ignoring the shouting of the attendant telling me to leave my card, ignoring everything but Jag's receding figure as I desperately try to keep him in focus. Brooklyn, unlike most areas, does not have heavy, milling crowds around the Transporter stage. This may be because there is less transit here than to most, because it is taken as a matter of course, or simply because Brooklyn is no longer populated by those who see any advantage in pursuing the tourists. As he races down the rubbled streets I am able to keep him in line, the thick, heavy light from the complexes casting pools which he dodges, in the light, out of the light, his body merely an apparition, and it is now as if there are only the two of us in this blasted place, although this cannot possibly be. Perhaps it is merely that my concentration is so intense.

'Stop it!' I shout as he runs in and out of the light. 'Jag, stop it! I only want to talk!' but these shouts merely accelerate the desperation of his run, and I know that I must have been right; my instincts were correct all the time: he was going to Final Trip on this very shift and was waiting around the landing stage to do it in Brooklyn. Why else would he have reacted with such terror? 'Stop it!' I shout again, and as if my voice was a rope cast at great distance he seems to jerk, shudder in the air, and then he collapses to the stones whimpering, grasping an ankle. Furiously I close the ground, coming in on him with only a few yards in separation, and then I fall to the ground myself, an ankle wrenched, feeling the stones collide underneath my feet. We have run clear into a bomb field, one of the unrestored from the Peril, that is clear, and now, like fools, the two of us are whimpering in these ashes, Jag holding his leg, my own

57

ankle sending flashes of blue pain to my head. 'You fool,' I say to him, 'you fool.'

He looks across at me, his eyes luminous in the darkness. 'I think I've broken my leg,' he says.

'You haven't,' I say. 'You can't; it's impossible,' but it is as if I already know that he is right. He has broken his leg and I my ankle; two fools in the rubble. 'I merely wanted to talk to you,' I say hoarsely. My ankle feels a little better; there is a shade of articulation, and I am able to talk through and around the pain. 'You didn't have to run.'

'You broke my leg for me,' Jag says.

'No I didn't,' I say. 'I couldn't; if I had broken your leg, you wouldn't even be able to talk, you'd be in so much pain. Come on,' I say, putting my hands firm to the rubble, dragging myself upright. A thousand pins prick my palms, but I am standing, the ankle holding the weight. 'Come on,' I say, 'you can do it. Your leg isn't broken. You're fine.' I feel desperate; part of my urgency is from indecision as to what I will do if he is indeed incapacitated. What is there to do? The logic, of course, is simply to leave him, since he has wanted to die anyway, but logic did not motivate the decision to pursue.

'Come on,' I say again, 'you can do it,' and extend a hand toward him. Jag seizes it; his two damp hands like loaves of bread encircle mine, and then, groaning, he pulls himself upright, plants his leg, moves slightly with the other, then repeats the gesture.

'It's all right,' he says. 'It isn't broken. I can walk.'

'I told you,' I say. 'I told you it was all right. Let's get out of here.'

'Why did you follow me?'

'Why did you run?'

Jag shakes his head. There is plenty of light; I can see him distinctly. 'That is none of your business,' he says. 'You should not have followed me.'

'You can't Final Trip. I won't let you.'

'Oh yes you will,' Jag says, breaking into a shambling walk. 'Oh yes you will. I can do anything I want; we're permitted and you encouraged me. Remember, you were the first – '

'That was before,' I say, ' – that was before what has happened; I can't let you do it now.'

'Why?' He weaves before me, puts out his hands to settle himself, little reflections of the pain cutting across his face.

'You can't stop me; I can do anything I want. It's my life – '

'No,' I say, 'no, we're all tied together, all of our lives. Let's go back to the Transporter.'

'I can't move.'

'Yes you can,' I say. I wedge a hand in his armpit, force him into a wavering stride surrounded by gasps. 'You can do it if you want to.' He shudders in posture – then, as if falling would be too much trouble, would only invoke further pain, begins to move in a shambling stride. Lights play amidst the rubble; from little spaces in the buildings I can see faces peering. From way down, shouts begin. 'Come on,' I say, 'run.' There are hoots in the darkness.

'Run?' Jag says. 'I can't run. I can't move,' but this is merely rhetoric; in truth he begins to move very quickly, breaking into a rapid hobble. 'You're crazy,' he says, stroking a hand across his forehead. 'You've got to be crazy.'

Sounds are spilling out from the corridors behind the street now. The pain in my ankle has gone away; I seem to be moving suspended in the air. 'Don't talk,' I say, 'just run.'

'Crazy,' Jag says again. 'This is crazy.'

We are moving rapidly now. It is impossible to gauge the distance back to the Transporter, but it must be several kilometers that we covered in our weaving run, and suddenly the street is covered with forms; ahead of us there is a solid line of people still not distinguishable in the darkness, holding themselves across our path. 'For God's sake,' Jag says, 'look at that.'

'I'm looking,' I say, but in truth I am not looking at all but running head-on into them, and at some perilous instant just before I feel they are about to see us and break the line, run at us, I dodge into a sudden maw which has opened up to the right, dragging Jag inside with me, and there the two of us stand, sodden, gasping, in a small space which has the damp odor of stone. I can hear the curl and choke of Jag's breath, and suddenly the unreasonableness of the situation breaks over me: what are the two of us doing here in Brooklyn, fleeing from a mob which we imagine is out to destroy us, when none of this had to be, when we could be back at Dance? We make our struggles for ourselves; we are creatures who simply cannot bear stasis. 'I shouldn't have told anyone,' Jag is whimpering. 'If I hadn't told anyone, it wouldn't have been this way;

59

you wouldn't have followed me here, I wouldn't have hurt my leg, it wouldn't be like this – '

'You had to tell,' I say. 'And besides, what does it matter? What are you babbling about? You wanted to F.T. – well, here's your chance; why are you afraid now?' and he starts to whimper again, something about choosing and selecting the means of your departure which are even more important than the fact of the departure itself, but I put a hand on his arm and yank him to silence. In the sliver of light outside our place we can see the forms appearing; they flood past us, shutting off the light, and for an instant I think they are going to see us, come into the alley and seize us, but they pass onward. Old tales of Brooklyn now pass across consciousness: third-hand reports of massacres and violence, roving packs living not in complexes but in rubble, disintegrated fragments of humanity looting and pillaging, living flat to the land rather than far above it, and what they must do to express their rage and alienation, all of this as spewed out in the courses on urbanization, a dark, blood wetness in my loins, the loins quivering, opening and closing as I think about this and what they might do next . . . but nothing happens, nothing happens whatsoever; the flickers of light open up into that long, slow graceful infusion, and there is nothing in the corridor then but the sound of Jag's breathing purring down my back.

'We're safe,' he says. 'I think we're safe now.'

'Wait,' I say, 'and wait,' and we do so; we stand in that alley for a very long time, pressed against each other, the light streaming. It falls evenly against us, and after a long time even I am willing to concede that somehow we have come through and that the pack will not return.

'My leg is still sore,' Jag whispers. 'I don't think it's right,' but I do not listen to this. I tug him insistently; he follows, limping, and slowly we move out into the open space again and back toward the Transporter, Jag hobbling behind.

'You know something?' he says. 'I wasn't frightened. Toward the end I wasn't frightened at all but ready. I didn't care.'

'You can't do it,' I say, referring to the Final Trip, 'can't do it,' but there is a sudden stab of revulsion. I simply do not want to talk about it anymore, do not want to get into any of it, and we only return to the Transporter, through the desultory observers to the side, and feed ourselves into it, to return to Dance.

Nothing has happened. Jag has not committed the Final Trip, nor have I dissuaded him, nor have the packs gotten to us. Nothing has happened at all.

Is it possible that we are living in a world devoid of event? Was *this* Cage's vision?

XII

And so, then, on one of the shifts that fall sometimes between Jag's decision to try the Final Trip and that bright terrible moment when I find that he has done so, the news carried back and forth through the passageways in the traditional means of announcement; before that declaration of intention and that seizing instant when I realize that he has done it and that that instant of connection must have been framed immutable from the time of declaration; he had moved upon it then and no one to stop him – in one of the shifts that fall midway between these two points graphed out on the chart that is the life of Jag . . . I am visited by the government man, in my cubicle, as I must have always known it would be.

The government man is a small, cool cat in frayed threads who is trying to preserve elements of control and authority as he addresses me. I can understand his position. He comes from the government, and the government which controls all our lives must show its own kind of discipline; he, its representative, then. But after only a short while his coolness impacts on him; it begins to chip away, his threads start to congeal on the sweating panels of his body . . . and he no longer is a slender, dapper little cat performing an interview but a dream figment, one of my own celebrated dead, I would think if I did not know better, who is trying to hold to the empty pieces of his control.

Since we have returned from Brooklyn, Jag has been sullen, has avoided contact with me, just as I have with Sherry. Inside I want to think that in some hard way he has changed, but I am not sure of this; most probably the intention itself remains. The government man has nothing to do with this, though. His understanding would not involve Brooklyn or the use of the Transporter; he is in the here and now.

'This has to do with the matter of Jagway,' he says, leaning against a wall, 'a person in your Survival Group.'

'I have no name to call you.'

'It is not necessary for you to call me any name whatsoever.'

'I do not do well without names,' I say. This is the best way to shake government men, or for that matter leaders; force a naming upon them and they no longer feel that they have no identity.

'Call me anything you wish,' he says; 'it does not matter.'

'My name is Sid. Sometimes I am known as Slick Sid, but usually I am known as nothing.'

'I don't care what your name is. This refers to Jagway.'

'Talk to him then.' I do not like government men. I have never seen any reason why I should. The lives they occupy are meaningless, but their power to damage is absolute. Fortunately, they do most often keep to themselves. 'Confidences of the Group are absolute,' I say. It is near the end of the shift, and had my intention been to visit Trinidad once more, now the government man has interfered with this neat and simple plan. I keep my fury in check, however. Only trouble can come from those who would argue with them.

'Not when they pertain to suicide.'

'They pertain to everything.'

'New regulations,' the government man says. He extracts a pamphlet from his pocket, shows me something in writing. 'These are exempted.'

'Put it away. I don't comprehend reading. I don't approach written matter.'

'Accept the assurance,' he says, putting it away inside himself, removing a large blank book and a pen, balancing the book on his knee. 'I want you to tell me what you know.'

'I know nothing.'

'Jagway is not authorized to suicide.'

I laugh at him. 'Everybody is authorized to suicide, I say.'

'Not anymore, I tell you. Suicide is now impermissible.'

'I haven't heard it.'

'You will hear it,' the government man says grimly. It occurs to me for the first time during this interview that he is actually serious. He believes Final Tripping to be against the codes; he is seeking information. 'Everyone will hear it. And even under the older codes it was never to be encouraged under any circumstances. We have information that it is being encouraged in your Group.'

'That is absolute nonsense,' I say.

'It may be nonsense, but these are the reports we have. I seek information.'

How foolish! How stupid! It would be difficult to believe that any of this has been going n, that I am actually being interrogated about Jagway, who is seeking the Final Trip, except that it *is* happening, it does possess objective truth, and Sid has long since learned to trust his sense of reality. If something appears to be happening, then it therefore *is* occurring, unless, of course, it is not. This acceptance of extrinsic reality has been one of the guideposts of my life: it has enabled me to appropriate the car, possess Sherry, get rid of Sherry, go to Brooklyn to find Jag, save us from assault. Only for dreamers is there true disaster.

I shake my head, recline on the rough pallet which is my resting place when I am not in transit, and try, however laboriously, to feign a position of ease.

'You know that I can't talk about anything going on within the Group,' I repeat. 'All of these confidences are absolute.'

'The Survival Groups were codified by the government,' the man says. 'They were a creation for the benefit of the populace, settled by legislative fiat.' He appears to be quoting; most of their rote information is implanted by hypnotic techniques, or so I am led to understand. Actually the government is for me largely a mystery and I understand nothing. 'This puts them clearly within our province of investigation, all of them, and we are concerned with the acceleration of suicides in the Dance Sector.'

'They are legal.'

The government cat shakes his head. 'Suicide is a privilege,' he says, 'it is not a right. More and more it has been wrongly appropriated as such, but there is nothing in the written or unwritten law which settles upon it as a part of what is your life.'

'It is not our life. It is our death.'

'Don't be snide about his. I warn you that I am interviewing you as a true representative. Now,' he says, pleased with himself as if he has found the argument convincing; perhaps he came here without a settled point of view, 'I want you to tell me everything you know about Jagway. When did he first declare intent?'

I shake my head. Truly my cubicle has never seemed so oppressive. There does not seem to be the space for two of us here; one and a half is more like it; one of me and half a government man instead of the whole cat at whom I am staring. One half would be as much as I can handle, but sometimes in the absence of force, a simple determination will have the same effect of causing the foe to fall away. It is a lesson to be taken from many of the celebrated dead who were willing to express their will against often overwhelming opposition. 'I will not talk about this,' I say. 'I will add nothing. You have no right to force me. It would be against all the codes of the Group, which I understand, I know, and I cannot go against them.'

And saying this leads to a newer, more ominous thought even superimposed against his reply: is it possible there is a spy in the Group? Who is passing on these reports to them? How does the capital know of Jag's intention? What are they doing with information on intimate confidences given within that context? The only explanation must be that someone, perhaps the leader himself, is routinely turning over reports to the capital, but this is something I simply cannot accept. Does the government man also know of the stolen car, the unauthorized trips to 1-80, my quick and spiritless couplings? All of these, from time to time, have at least been alluded to. I am not sure that any of them, strictly speaking, are illegal, but then if something is personally satisfying, it is likely that the capital (or what is left of it; there are rumors that the government is functionless) is against it. I wish Kennedy (1917–1963) were around so that I could discuss it with him. Doubtless he would have some ideas on the subject.

'No sir,' I say, 'no sir, no sir, I cannot talk about any of this. Right or wrong, whatever your assurances, I cannot betray the compact of the Group. I am deeply sorry. I wish it were not this way. But you have got to understand my position; I must live on my own level.'

'Bastard,' the government man says. He puts away his papers with a growl, stands, looks at my little cubicle, revulsion popping into his eyes, and I see then that he hates me. Little flowers of sweat come out in petals across his forehead. I can look into sudden pores which in magnification would be canyons, would lead to the dense, dark spaces of his skull, where, trapped in bone, the brain is hanging, pulsing, gelatinous. In that ruined brain, thoughts like insects scurry as Jag and I did in the rubble of Brooklyn. The image is irresistible; I can escape it; in imagination I squeeze the government man's brain, and out of it comes a greenish fluid which leaves little messages of stain across the creases of his scalp. He reaches into his pocket and pulls out a small holograph.

'Look at this,' he says, 'I want you to look at it.'

I shake my head. I will touch nothing that he has held; I will also have a diseased and gelatinous brain. But he tosses it in the air quickly, and by instinct I swoop forward; before I know what has happened, I have trapped it in my hand. I feel the warmth penetrating.

'Look at it,' he says.

'No.'

'*Look at it,*' he repeats, and I do so, sickened, no way for me not to as my fingers come open and in my palm I see the tiny likeness of Jag suspended like a jewel in my hand.

'Is that him?' he asks. 'Is that Jagway? Tell me.'

I look at the holograph and it is Jag, the eyes perfectly miniaturized in the reduced shell of the face, the neck shaped like his neck but fleshed out subtly, a work of art, this, in addition to one of reproduction; the holographer was unable to resist the urge to bring Jag wholly into focus, and so it is not the stalk of his neck from which Jag's head hangs suspended but rather a delicate, well-formed one; the mouth too has a different cast, deeper, less thin, more joyous, and the nose has been leveled off against the planes of the cheekbones so that what I have in my hand at one-twentieth is an idealized Jag, a Jag transmogrified, the Jag That Could Have Been, and yet for all of this art it is still a likeness which I hold, a stunning testament to the will of the creator. Has the government done this for all of us? If they know so well what we are and how we could appear, why could they not do it for us? I shake my head and hold the holograph so that the government man may retrieve it, but he does not; he merely stares at me. 'Tell me,' he says, 'is it him?'

'I don't know. I told you that. I don't know anything about it.'

'Deny that this is him. Deny that this is the Jagway of whom we are speaking.'

So if I have seen into his brain, fair trade; the government man has seen into mine; he knows the poisonous secrets that are moving around in there, and yet desperately, holding on to my refusal as I had in the Church of the Epiphany looked for affirmation, I say, 'What do you want, what do you want me to say, what do you want of any of us?' I am weeping. 'I cannot defy the Group; it is the only thing which I have ever understood,' I say, and raise my arm to fling the holograph across the wall, but he is quicker than I am and blocks the gesture with an elbow, then slides his fingers up my arm and reappropriates the likeness. Shuddering, he replaces it inside himself.

'I am sorry,' he says, 'I am really sorry. I have tried to do this in a reasonable way, but you will not listen. None of you people will listen. You absolutely have to be brought to your senses.'

He reaches into another crevice of clothing and brings out a small, blunt weapon with a projective snout – a narcoticizer, I see instantly – and there is an explosive pain in my left antrum at the next instant, a pain that chokes off my sinuses immediately; I open my mouth, drawing breath, gasp and feel my own bile rise against me as, wind cut off, I sink to the floor. At least I can manage speech. 'No right,' I mumble, each word an intake of breath, and it must take me a long time to say this: 'You have no right to do it.'

He stands over me, looming, the snout held down. 'Extraordinary circumstances demand extraordinary measures.'

'Pain,' I say, 'pain . . . ' and something occurs to me then: the government is capable of doing anything. Despite the fact that I have never felt that the capital has anything to do with our lives, we live on their sufferance. If someone on the level of the government man is permitted to, is capable of doing such hings, then there is just no accounting at all for the government. I close my eyes and feel waves and waves of anguish hitting me, part from what he has done, part from what I am thinking. All of it was a lie; even the Transporter, the Final Trip, the illusion that we could come out of our lives, do anything we wish. They had other ideas for us. Always they permitted the illusion, but what was in hand, waiting, was the narcoticizer.

'You will recover gross motor control in five to ten minutes,' the government man says. 'The pain is already ebbing.' His voice sounds doubtful, but maybe it is because I am not hearing very well; then again it may be a simple astonishment at his own means. 'I regret this; I am truly sorry to have done it. Your kinesthetic sense will return. You will be well. In the meantime, you must now talk to me and answer my questions.'

'Bastard,' I say, but it is defeat, not defiance. 'Dirty bastard.'

'Listen to me,' he says and kneels to my level, extends the holograph again. 'Listen, and there need be no more pain. Everything is simple. Everything is almost finished. Is this Jagway?'

'Yes,' I say. I can get air now. It does not matter; I can say anything I want. 'Yes, that is him.' Blood pools in thick little clots of the legs; the body feels hollow above the waist, thick and damaged below. Is this death? Not the Final Trip but simply the well of death itself without the exaltation that is associated with release? My genitals feel luminous. I imagine that they are brightly burning from some hidden part which cannot be seen. 'I was trying to stop him,' I say. 'I did not want him to do it. I would have brought him around myself, I would have persuaded him not to do it, if only you had let – '

'When did he first mention his intention to suicide?'

'I don't remember. I do not remember.'

'Was it longer than five shifts ago?'

'I can't answer that,' I say desperately. 'The Group confidences . . . ' and then it falls away. It was dissimulation from the start; I myself did not believe in the confidence of the Group, or I never would have pursued him through the Transporter. Yes. Seeing this, it is as if some disgusting internal organ had been revealed to me for the first time, something like the gall-bladder or liver hidden behind the wall of skin, performing its unaccounted duties or lack of them in a bed of slime until a sudden flap was torn through the skin and I was led for the first time to confront . . . myself. I must live with what has been revealed. 'The hell with the Group,' I say, weeping. 'The Group means nothing.'

'Not for this it does not.'

'I believed in it. I really believed in it, but it doesn't matter. They lied. They lied to us, about everything.'

'Not everything,' the government man says. He sounds gentle; it is as if something has been torn open in him as well; shock has laid him open to the bone. 'Some things are still important. But this overrides the Group. The situation is serious, and it cannot be tolerated.'

'You always did. You gave us the Final Trip.'

'We did not understand what you had made of it. When did he first mention suicide? What did he say was the basis of it? What did he give as his motivation, and in what way did he intend to do it? Was it going to be a drug death? I know you are feeling better now. You are in no pain. So tell me. It's quite hopeless, you see. You can't resist any longer, and there's nothing *to* resist. Tell me what I want to know. Here,' he says, reaching forward, 'here, let me help you,' and gently he tugs me to an upright position, slides me delicately across the floor so that my back is propped against a wall. He kneels before me, and the seams of his face are tight, producing a smooth, gracious countenance. He looks like one of the Four Priests.

'Tell me,' he says.

All of my perceptions were wrong. I was wrong about everything. Through the network of pain which the narcoticizer has brought upon me but which is already, as promised, fading, I see him in a new perspective, and he is something very much like the way I could be, the way I might have been if matters had been different, if there is a difference still to be enacted. All of us are the same, only the institutions have control. If he were the devil he would have approached with a tongue of fire, not with a weapon to force the truth. Poor limited beings that we are, we can deal with one another through force; it is the only prop. The government speaks and the people hear, but the government knows no language, and the people no longer have ears. What I took to be weakness, what I thought was doubt peeping through the tattered shreds of passion in this man, is something else, something without a name. All of my life, then, all of my life I had seen the world one way, and it was really another; all of my life I had thought that it worked through leverage when it had always been the other way and it was sufferance.

I will never excuse myself. I will never excuse this lapse of understanding; it is unforgivable; still, there it is and nothing to be done about it. If it were to have been changed it would better have been done a long time ago and now I am down the tube, into the pipe and irretrievably cut off from that which I had once believed, to say nothing of whatever the truth of it might have been.

Biting my lips, shaking my head, I try yet one last time to hold out, to bring on the resistance which will save me and save Jag too . . . but I am defeated by my new desire, the desire to push the disaster yet one step further and be done with all of it. I can feel the dampness of that desire in all the pockets of self, and there is a violent implosion then. It rocks me. It comes from the inside and has nothing to do with the narcoticizer.

Clean, purifying, it cuts through me: I see that I can hold out no longer, nor do I see any necessity to do so. Why bother? The Transporter will be there; still, they cannot take that from me, and I will be able to stuff myself into Cage's genius and go anywhere I wish: Hawaii, Hong Kong, the Ramapos. If it is all the same, no matter, I will make it different. Freedom comes from inside the skull, not from without. Without there is nothing but the government man.

So I look at him then and I see the knowledge filter into him that he is about to get his wish. That his desire palpitates heavily before him like meat on a hook, sweating in fresh beads like jewels, and in his eyes too there is a kind of hesitancy which I can sense: now that he has it, does he truly want it? Can he, any more than I, deal with the unspeakable truth that awaits us?

In the crevices of his serious face as it opens to this knowledge I can see little faces, all of which might be Jag's, and strangely reassured by this comforting and friendly image, I begin at last and at first to speak.

XIII

Later, much later, after Jag is found smashed out and dead in quarters despite all the efforts of the government man, alert to the danger, to stop him, after the Group has been broken up and scattered through others in the wake of the leader's abrupt disappearance, after I have spent a terrible shift in Trinidad observing for the last time the rituals of the epiphany which drive me only to terrified bellows that force my ejection, after the valves on the Cadillac have melted into the engine block, the car destroyed, and in the wake of that mysterious fire the armory closed forever – after all of this, but before the newer and more terrible part of my life begins, I go to Sherry and say, 'I am sorry. I'm sorry for everything.' Her body is hard, congealed against itself and me, and even as I say this I know that everything that has happened is gone, but still I must do this; I must try. 'I'm sorry,' I say again.

She shakes her head. 'You told about Jag,' she says. 'Everyone knows that.'

'I had to,' I say. I cannot deny it. There is nothing to deny. 'They made me. If I hadn't it would have been worse. They would have gone to all the rest of you until one of you told and all of you would have suffered instead of just me. I saved you all of that.'

'You were the one who told.'

'All right,' I say, 'I was the one who told. But he F.T.'d out anyway. He got free. So does it matter? Does any of it matter?'

'It matters very much.' She has aged during this period, as have all of us, and all of the silliness and delicacy have been squeezed out. 'It matters to me.'

'I am sorry. I wanted to say that I am sorry.'

'I will never see you again. I want you to get away from me. If you try to see me again, I will get out of Dance.'

'It didn't have to be this way,' I say. 'I didn't want it to be. I thought it was better for all of us to do it in that way.'

'I will never see you again. I want you to get away from me. If you try to see me again I will get out of Dance.'

'What difference does it make?' I say. 'All of the time we thought it was our lives, and it was merely theirs. We live inside them; we are merely dreams which they have created for our convenience. Cannot we at least be with one another?'

'I will never see you again. I want you to get away from me. If you try to see me again, I will – '

'All right,' I say, 'all right then, it doesn't matter. It's all over. It's finished.'

'I will never see you again,' she says, and I realize that she is a machine; they have made her a machine, as that is the only way, finally, that they can defeat me here too. 'I want you to get away . . . '

I turn, go from her cubicle. Perhaps she is still talking, but most likely she is not. The devices are clever. They would shut her off the moment it was no longer necessary for her to speak. They are efficient. They would not waste the energy. I go through the network of Dance and return to my cubicle. I am not weeping. There is nothing to weep about. I merely did what had to be done. Someone had to do it. The option of the Final Trip is yet mine to take. If I am quiet about it. I must be very quiet about it.

I put it to one side. There is plenty of time to deal with that later. There is no urgency; I will have that choice for the rest of my life. It is important to distinguish between that in which

70

choice is still left and that in which it is gone. For Sherry it is gone. For life it is open.

I return to my cubicle, and there through the night, through many nights, I converse with my celebrated dead, all of them coming to greet me with the walls down: Spinoza, Shakespeare, Cross, Goethe, Welber, Stearn, Lincoln, Casals, so many, and now that they know I am truly one of them, they are less officious, almost friendly, awkward in their friendliness as they discuss their lives with me, and I understand that in their shy, strange, desiccated ways (after all, most of them have been dead for a long time) they are merely trying to bid me greeting.

PART 2

I

So I am assigned then to go into the Dance Sector. After all this time, for reasons which I will never understand, they have decided to investigate the matter of the Final Trips. Two-thirds of them in Dance, verging on three-quarters, are doing away with themselves by the twenty-fifth year of their lives, the first year of their option; and at higher levels of the capital, we are told, they are curious. It is not so much that they want to cut off the suicides as that they want to understand why: why are so many of the unoptioned making such a drastic decision? Haven't they got enough to live for? Don't they want to make a real contribution? It is my belief – not that I think my belief means anything – that the capital is merely sulking. It is not so much that they cannot spare the suicides. Relief on population pressure, by any means, is to be accepted. But that two-thirds to three-quarters might suicide out rather than take their place under the capital . . . *this* makes them petulant. In any event, the project has begun. We are to define the reasons for this, and while we are making definition, we are to stop them in any way we can.

The project, we are instructed, has reached a high level of priority. It has been a subject of discussion for a long time, but there has always been more urgent business: shortages, riots, holding the base together, improving the life styles and the covenants in the complexes. From time to time the suicide question has been raised; we have been encouraged to include inquiries on motivations on investigation of all the dead, but there has always been something to intervene, and the pressures have not been for solution. One can hardly blame them. It is perfectly clear that they have not wanted to know.

One has that faith in the capital. Certainly I have it; they must know what they are doing, because they have been able, always, to rule. Circumstance carries its own weight; control is its own motivation. But even when one has fully accepted this, when one knows that he has gone through the tube of his life and nothing will ever change . . . that is precisely the moment at which the serious questioning must begin again. The perversity of them! Still, one can understand their position. The suicides are beginning to get out of control. In some of the complexes it is running over ninety percent. In Dance, certain sectors have been at ninety-five. By the simple rule of geometrics this would give the capital nothing to control within two generations. Hence their anxiety.

Into the circuit room, then, for my conference with Lance. Looking at him, I can see myself in thirty years – not that there is thirty years' physical difference between us. He is beaten, I am beaten: I feel that if either of us had had it to do over again, we would have suicided out ourselves rather than go on this way. Still, in some of us, the mad animal of hope scuttles uncaged: it has nothing to do with choice but only biology. Resentful survivors, Lance and I would have died with curses. One must accept one's life. One must accept what one has become.

'We've got a report from a Group head over in Dance,' Lance said. In certain ways I take him to be not only a projection but a reflection of myself: the same grayness, the same fine apprehension lurking in the corners of the eyes. Is it possible that we are indeed the same person? But I must repress thoughts like this; autism is dangerous, a sign of psychopathology. 'We're going to follow it through, take it all the way.'

'What?' I said, although I already knew via tape and memo what was coming next. There are no surprises. The environment must be controlled for Lance, the full program of the discussion, before he will ever begin. Knowing that he has these structures ahead of him permits him to go on. Who am I to criticize? Thirty years is nothing. I should have Finaled out myself, but at the last moment I failed of courage, and now it is too late. So I work for the capital.

'This kid has declared intention to suicide out.'

'That's nothing exceptional.'

'It's a random case, though. We've got him from the point of origin. Instead of picking them up in the middle, we can begin tracking where we should, right at the beginning. Don't you think so?' Lance said. 'Don't you agree with that?'

'I agree with everything.'

'The reports are here in hand. He's twenty-two years old, profiled to the absolute,' Lance said, looking down at some papers in his hand – showing no inclination, however, to pass them over. Once again, the assertion of control.

'Good,' I said, 'good. So he's declared intention to suicide out. Where do we go from there? He's one in a thousand.'

Lights danced like jewels from the surfaces of the circuit room; Lance rubbed his hands underneath them. I had never realized what a physically repellent man he was; brutality and awkwardness, a real *unkindness* as well. Defensive, of course, but what difference to it? Ultimately all results the same. The quick deadly smell of ozone started the throbbing once again in the frontal lobes of the head, dull intimations of unease starting, penetrating along the back. My distaste for physical pain – simple cowardice, perhaps – might explain my failure to suicide when metaphysically I always accepted all of its advantages. Terror disguised as courage. 'Is it a random case?'

'Yes, it's a random case. It could have been anyone. Dance is a good one to start pulling from, though. They're running ninety percent recently.'

'Then maybe we should have gone elsewhere. Factors may be slanted toward suiciding; it may be a subculture.'

'Crap,' Lance said, 'stupid crap. Dance is running ninety, the others seventy-two, seventy-three; that only means that Dance is less dysfunctional. All of the pressures are toward suicide.'

'Okay,' I said agreeably, 'so all of the pressures are toward suicide. I don't disagree with any of that. It's still random.'

'Of course it is. But there's a difference. We're going to find out why.'

'Are we?'

'We're going to track this one from the beginning,' Lance said, hitting his charts. 'I want this boy interviewed. I want a depth interview, hypnotics if necessary, but first I want all of the contacts. Everyone in his Group. I want to know why.'

'Why it's happening?'

'Why we can't stop them.'

'I don't know,' I said. 'I don't know why I can't stop them.'

'The technicians will, if we can give them the answers. We're going to profile this one to the depths; we're going to know everything about him. His name is Jagway.'

'It's still random,' I said, trying to be professional. 'Whatever you get may turn out to be a hypothesis on the curve. You might have a typical or an atypical; once you start on the depths, though, you'll never know either way.'

Lance shrugged. 'That's up to them. Those were the instructions. Let's let them decide where he fits in on the curve. I'm doing what I can with what we were given.'

'So I'm supposed to hit the field and cobble up a background,' I said.

'In depth.'

'Find out why he's decided to do it, what there is that brought him this way.'

'That's exactly what you're supposed to do.' He stood and walked over to the monitors, rested a hand on them, froze into position. At times like these I think Lance is merely posturing, but then again he may take all of this seriously. He is an essential mystery; all of us are. One will never know. 'And you're supposed to do it quickly.'

I stood myself, went over to join him. Heat glinted in the coils; I could feel it rising through the wires as I laid a hand down, the hand only inches from his, wondered what would happen if, shockingly, I were to cover the palm. Nothing. He would hurl me to the ground. Nothing would happen at all; we function merely within the role divide. I know this, but it does not make the lapse less painful; I wonder what would happen if we were not given the integrity of our own skulls. 'You know what we'll find?' I asked. 'Do you?'

'Let that be their concern.'

'We'll find a perfect randomness to pick up on your random sample. We'll find that he's doing it for reasons that can't be duplicated by anyone else. Don't you understand? There are an infinite number of reasons for suiciding out.' And only one

76

for staying alive, I think, but I suppress this. It would not lead to anything. All of us who have passed beyond the stage of option know what has kept us there; it is a horrid secret that does not need to be shared. We share it merely by living together. 'You'll look for a universal and find a particular.'

'I'm not looking for anything. They'll do the looking on this one. Let them worry about it.'

'Responsibility begins below,' I said. I felt contentious for reasons I could not understand; perhaps it was simply knowing that Lance was uncomfortable. Rarely is he such; his assurance is a thick gloss laid over the open spaces of his personality. 'If we won't make that decision, then neither will they. So it all comes down to us.'

'Listen,' Lance said and looked at the board: little circuits twinkling, each of them a life, some of them already dead – impossible to tell; that was the mystery of the lights – 'you don't seem to understand what it means to them.'

'I understand well enough. It's been going on for as long as we know.'

'Still, two-thirds of them are killing themselves before they're twenty-five. That means that two-thirds are going straight down the chute.'

'We didn't, did we?'

'We are not the norm.'

'That's for sure. That's for damned sure. Still, two-thirds, three-quarters of them are going down the chute all the way. We're not getting a useful quotient out of them.'

'Not *we*. *They*.' I could not explain my mood, but it felt dangerous, on the verge of the unspeakable. I had not known that such thoughts existed before. It was refreshing but also frightening.

'We are they. The two are inextricable. Now we've got a generation that's suiciding out from Dance to Brightside, all over, and if it's getting along like this,' he said, looking down at the charts wavering in his hands, 'well, if it goes on like this, we're not going to have a population left.'

'Why did they pull it off the shelf?'

'What?'

'This has been around as long as I can remember. The suicide question. Why have they decided to take another try at the same damned project? They could have done this anytime they wanted. Why don't they face up to the truth?'

'What truth?' Lance said. 'What truth are you talking about?' His eyes squinted at me. 'I'm not understanding you, Jorg.'

Say it and be damned. 'Maybe they don't have to fan us into the field to find an explanation. Maybe that explanation lies within myself.'

If I had thought that this would have some effect upon him, I was wrong; Lance crumpled within himself, little twitches moving up and down his back, and then bent over one of the circuits, watching it, the patterns of the lives. 'That's insupportable, Jorg,' he said. When my name is used repetitively it is a sign that I am moving into him on some vague, personal level, but little satisfaction can be derived from that. 'That kind of reasoning is insupportable.'

'It was just an idea,' I said, and felt myself beginning to move in retreat. Go forward, go back; I will never follow a proposal through to its logical outcome. It is certainly a defect, but cowardice has so many ramifications that that is the least of them. 'Is there anything more to say? I'd like to go if there isn't.'

Tentatively I reached toward the chart he held in his hand, touching it, feeling its weight slick under the fingertips, and he yanked it back from me, the chart flapping like a wing; he stumbled, nearly fell into a circuit. 'Fool,' he said. 'Jorg, you're a fool.'

'I just wanted to look at it.'

'For what you've said and what you were doing you could be sent away from here. Do you want that? Do you want an investigation?'

'I don't want anything,' I said, and it was almost true. It was close enough to the truth to be indistinguishable from it; I should have left it there, not wanting anything. It is a better way to consider most questions. 'I'm not here to argue,' I said. 'I'm not here to disrupt. I thought you would give me the chart and I could begin to do some checking, that was all.' My tone was sniveling, ingratiating; listening to myself I was appalled. Still, what can one do? Positions control our lives.

Lance said, 'Jorg, this is the last time.' He ran his hand over the metal, seemed to derive comfort from it. 'It's the last time I'll permit talk like this without putting in a report.'

'All right. I'm sorry.'

'To an extent I'm willing, all of us are willing, to accept you. We come from the same Group. But this is not sufficient.

Apologies are not sufficient, and this is truly dangerous.'

'Okay,' I said, extending a hand. 'I know that. I said that I was sorry. Give me the chart; let me take it back for a study.'

Reluctantly he allowed it to pass from his hand to mine, and I knew I had won. Although, won what? This is always the question one must encounter. 'I'll check it through,' I said and turned from him, tucking the chart under an arm. 'I'll see what I can discover. I'll see what I can report.'

'Wait,' Lance said, and I turned toward him. In his hand he held a bright object with many circumstances. A holograph.

'This is the subject,' Lance said. 'Study it.' As he put it into my hand, I felt the gnarled surfaces stroke like fire. 'That's for you. The chart I want you to return, but this you are to keep. To take out into the field. For verification and identity.'

'All right,' I said, 'all right,' squeezing the little object – it gave me back faint resilience – and stuffing it into a pocket. Nicholas Jagway. Nicholas N. Jagway, twenty-two years old. I went to the door, reached for the knob, got it open.

'Jorg?' Lance said, and I turned toward him to see that he was looking at me intensely; the masks of our conversation had fallen away, and he was now the man he had been twenty years ago when we had decided with each other not to do it. 'Jorg, do it right. Don't go wrong with this one. We can't spare them. We cannot spare them anymore.'

'I know,' I said, although I did not know, and, clutching the chart, that talisman, the holograph bumping in a pocket against my genitals, got out of there.

II

In my cubicle, poring over the charts, I assume an identification with Jagway. This is a familiar phenomenon; on any case, sooner or later, there is this feeling of blending, merging with the subject, so that the two of us become one, and from that extraordinary sensitivity (of which I am not proud) the investigation becomes more fluid.

Jagway, twenty-two years old, appears before me. His body is slightly wasted by overuse of mediums, but otherwise is reasonably well-nourished for a male of his age. Upon me he turns eyes of luminous blue. 'Come on,' he says, 'join me.'

'I can't.'

'Sure you can. Anybody can. Wouldn't you like to take the Final Trip?' He makes a cutting motion across his throat, winks. 'You'll love it. It's the best there is.'

'We don't call it Final Tripping in the Department. We call it suicide.'

'Call it what the fuck you want to,' Jagway says, 'it's still a great thing.' He coughs; his face convulses. 'Best thing in the world.'

'But why?' I say to him, a naïve question, but an investigation must begin at the point of naïveté, curving through that, then to the darker corners. 'Why do you want to do it?'

'Why not? It's great. It's the only thing going. Don't you want to?'

'Leave me out of it. I'm merely the investigator.'

'But you've got to get personally involved. Don't give me that investigation shit; that's just a cover. Hell, you want to do it, don't you?'

'Stop it!'

'Of course you want to do it,' Jagway says. 'I can see it in your eyes. I can see when somebody wants to Final Trip bad, just like you do.'

'I won't discuss it anymore.' I apply myself to the charts. Somewhere within is the secret that enables me to control him.

Jagway seizes the charts and throws them against the wall. Paper flaps. 'Stupid bastard,' he says, 'you missed your chance, that's all. You're envious. You wish you had done it.'

'Get out of here.'

'I can't,' he says absently; 'you were the one who brought me in. Face it, the only reason you're on this is that you didn't want to do it yourself way back and you don't know why. You think I can show you the reasons, you can find out for yourself. Get some understanding.'

'Enough,' I say. 'I don't want to listen to this anymore.' I go to the corner, begin to stab at the charts, pick them up, straining. When I come erect Jagway is there, leering at me.

'Stupid old bastard,' he says, 'there isn't a one of you who wouldn't do it if he had the chance. You just want to get out of yourselves.'

And this is so infuriating, having to listen to this from a subject, real or imagined, that for the second time I hurl the charts at the wall and then turn to engage Jagway, but of course he is gone, as I could have expected, and I have no one but myself to conjure with as I begin, slowly, to come to terms with the fact that of all the investigations, this will be the most difficult and dangerous of all . . . and I would not be surprised if Lance had put me on it deliberately, so great his perversity, so capricious his understanding.

I continue to study the charts, now obsessed. After what has happened I will not permit him to evade me.

III

Dance has a reputation as the most dangerous and diseased of all the complexes, but I have always felt that Rockland, which was my own in pre-orientation, was even more difficult. Rockland was gutted in the explosions of the late twenties, and there is little evidence now of what it was, but in its time it was remarkable, perhaps the most diseased and desperate of complexes (retrospection is a heightening and a sharpening; everything in retrospection must be an absolute; otherwise why bother recollecting it? But it *was* terrible), so far removed from what I have come to understand subsequently as the world that it was even cut off from the Transporter. I was twelve before I got into a Transporter for the first time, and that was an experience to wrench one's bones, but is a different recollection for a different place: what matters here is that I have not been to Rockland for three years, and the last time I went was the first for ten before *that*; even so, it all swept upon me, the dread and depression of those old buildings coming upon me in thick winds and waves which were an instant and grim reconstruction not only of the geography but of the *mood* of my youth, and when I left, it was knowing that I would not return. Strangely, however, it seems to remain viable for many who live there. The faces which I saw did not seem to be notably depressed; not any more than mine was. Of course life from the inside out may appear different. Brooklyn holds satisfaction for some of its tenants as well.

But out of Rockland, into the Transporter, past the point where I could have suicided out, my only desire was to stay as far from it as possible, and now that desire has been achieved. The same must be true for Lance, although I have never discussed it with him. There is really nothing to discuss, but between us there is a basic, unstated point that must be acknowledged: that the percentage of suicides in Rockland was lower than in most surrounding complexes and still, even now, remains relatively stable at somewhere around fifty percent. Fifty percent of Rocklanders seem, despite all they have been through, to find life necessary, to find it supportable. It is a mystery but one which Lance and I can never acknowledge.

Seeing Jagway in the magnification of tunnel vision, I see a little bit of myself, but it is inexplicable, and I know that this knowledge, whatever its merit, would not enable me to touch him.

IV

To Trinidad I take myself then. Somewhere lies an answer to all of this, but it is not to be found here; maybe in Trinidad, then. Putting Jagway's charts to one side, putting aside the difficulties of the shift and my own gloomy, glowing perception that at the end of this I will find something of myself which would be better undiscovered, I feed myself into the Transporter, pop into the steaming, disordered streets coming like arteries from the stage. Trinidad exists only for, only because of, the Transporter, and that is good, but I know that I have limited myself by seeing so much of it, and that I should try to extend myself in other directions. Sometime I will do this. In the meantime, I settle for the possible; it can take a lifetime simply to get to that point.

As I work my way through the screaming streets, beggars waving their fists at me, little pieces of soul and scrap seem to be missing, left behind in the machinery, which I will never find again. Every trip through reduces me somewhat; from the Transporter, regardless of its efficacy, I take a feeling of loss, something irretrievable having vanished down that chute forever, some part of me never to be found again, the familiar illusion of the Transporter and, for all I know, a true one. Over the years I feel that little bits and pieces of me have been trailed from Hong Kong to Jakarta, Spuyten, to the engines of Madrid, and of that basic core material with which all of us start out, I may, perhaps, have seventy-five percent left: the

82

question is, what is the irreducible minimum below which we cannot fall and still be human? . . . but there is no point in worrying about this. It makes no difference. One handles adjustments, in and out of this world, as well as one can. No better. And no worse.

Trinidad is the place to be in these last shifts before the pursuit of Jagway begins. It forms a perfect correlative to my own sense of decomposition, long there, increasing since I found that I was able to summon Jagway's specter. On these streets I am assaulted by beggars, hookers, young boys, young girls, old people waving streamers, great orange pennants, in the air which declaim various entertainments, officials wearing the dull blue of the supervisory class who look upon all of this unhappily. Trinidad has become primarily a problem in traffic management. A child, sex indeterminate, rubs against my knee, and then as I bend looks up with a strangely triumphant expression. 'Dirty, filthy son of a bitch, you're doomed,' it says distinctly and then merges into the crowds. The crowds swarm.

I have no time to be distracted by any of this. Not even by the child; curses from strangers have not concerned me for a long time; I must bear under my own curses. *Ne sala, ne sala*, I cry in universal as I cut through the colors, *I will not participate.* As I move from the central network into those barren places behind the city itself, only a few meters from the landing stage, it is open country once again. The cluster is all front, all demonstration; Trinidad breaks into dirt close to its great stage, and the dirt leads to corridors of this place where no one from the Transporter has ever walked.

And here the landscape looks as it might have looked hundreds of years ago. Nothing has changed. I prowl my way through meters and meters, the crowds falling away, and then the ruins begin to lose color, even energy being drained from these artifacts; nothing but mere gray slabs pressed into the Earth, warrens in which humans are stacked in levels, and it is horrid to think of that subterranean population going into the ground. This is not the way men should live; men should live piled atop one another, moving upward into heaven. But this was most economic for them. Now faint images of lust are beginning to claw at me with their birdlike little limbs; I feel heat beginning to emanate from the panels of the body. How long, O Lord, how long? But one must be patient; this burden too will be taken from me.

From one of those flat constructions a group of boys burst, apparently in hiding, waiting for a lone passerby. I put my hand into my pocket, feeling for my weapon, but their intentions are not aggressive; they are, it seems, merely the sentries. *Ah cwai!* one of them shouts, *return!* and they fall away, then back into the little patches of night which have disgorged them, and as quickly as they were here, so they are gone, and the boy and I confronting each other in the empty place. He looks at me intently. 'As before?' he says.

'As before.'

'It will be the same.'

'That is how I want it.'

'Good,' he says, 'good,' and we exchange solemn, collaborative nods. Our eyes lock; he must be sixteen, no older, seventeen perhaps, his eyes small animals afire in his skull. He turns, begins to walk. I follow him at a distance, listening to the scattering sound I hear in the Earth, a sound of movement, displacement, watching, too, the small, hard circle of his buttocks which semaphore their odd and convoluted message. I have never thought of it. My desires, limited at best, have never tended in that direction. I simply would not know what to do with him, or so I assure myself is the case.

Down a ruined line we go, grotesque wooden parodies of old houses on our side, and he pauses before one of them without light, waits for me to catch up with him and extends his hand, pointing. 'It is here now,' he says.

'Here? It was – '

'It was necessary to change it.'

'But there is no light – '

'Inside,' the boy says, 'inside there will be light,' with a dark circumstantial knowledge which I have never possessed, which I wish I could have. 'Inside light,' he says again and extends a hand.

'Is it all right?' I say. There is a hesitancy in my tone which disgusts me, but I must go forward, expose to him my vulnerability. 'Because if there is not, then – '

'We have changed,' the boy says, 'but everything remains the same,' his hand still held out, and seeing that there is nothing more I can do with him, that I have in some way pushed him far more than I should have, even now I go to my own pocket, take out exchange, put it in his hand. His hand closes over it like machinery, he jams it into a pocket and then

84

runs. One moment I can hear his steps in the darkness and then I cannot. So quickly is transfer arranged in Trinidad.

Now I can only hope that I have not been made a fool; that this is not a blind. I go into the antique doorway, raise my hand to pound, then find that it has instead fallen unbidden to the knob, and I turn it in my hand, move into the hallway. And in that hallway I have at last returned to the familiar, and I move deftly, quickly into a larger room in which an enormous woman looks at me, swathed not only in her flesh but in an assurance so profound that I would not even know its name. At one time she might have been gaunt, and still that thinness prevails; the flesh is extraneous. 'Ah,' she says, 'it is you again.'

'Yes,' I say.

'I thought you would return.'

'Oh yes,' I say, 'oh yes, I knew I would.'

'So many do not, but you we can count on, eh? Is that right?'

'Oh yes,' I say, 'you can count on it,' and there is a pause during which we say nothing; she returns to a corner of the room and stands there. On a turntable a small holograph of Oplaus rotates slowly, the feet in their gnarled position; the tiny mouth, exquisitely formed, seems on the verge of epiphanic chant. A stirring likeness. Little shafts of colored light come from the turntable on its promenade; I glare at it, fascinated, and wonder what Oplaus is doing here. What precisely is the significance? Two matters of epiphany, of course, but the woman does not seem at that level of irony. I would never discuss it with her; certain things cannot be.

'Is she available?' I say.

The woman shrugs. Oplaus turns peaceably. 'Sometimes she is,' she says, 'and sometimes she is not. It depends.'

'I hope she is available.'

'We all hope. We live in a single condition of hope all our lives, never in a present.' She moves with sudden birdlike grace to the door. 'We will have to see. That is all that we can do.'

'Yes,' I say, my voice suddenly trapped within my throat. 'Yes, we will have to do that.'

She moves behind curtains. I stand there, looking at Oplaus, until I realize that I am verging on hypnotic absorption, and I wrench my eyes away, turning them to the ceiling, the walls, all of the facets of the room. Somewhere at the rim of consciousness I am pondering Jagway and Lance. In certain ways they are the same; in other ways they are different. But they will never conjoin. This thought, vaguely irrational, is tantalizing at the same time, and I burrow through it, meditating, the woman coming through the curtains again to make an encouraging gesture. 'She is available,' she says.

'Good.'

'She will be waiting for you in the third room to the left.'

Here they still say 'room' instead of 'cubicle'. Utterly familiar, utterly alien; there is no way to come to terms with what they truly represent. 'Thank you,' I say.

'Before you go, it is necessary for you to pay me. You recall that from the last time.'

'Oh yes,' I say, 'I recall from the last time,' and from the time before that and the time before *that*, these occurrences stretching back murkily over a long period, but she apparently can grasp nothing more than the concept of *last*, just as my own recollection fails at a point a little earlier than that, and who is to say there is any difference? Who could say that I am superior to her? 'Here,' I say, and take more exchange from my pocket, 'I hope that will be sufficient.'

She looks at it, counts it laboriously as I spread it in my hand, then hesitantly takes it. 'It looks proper.'

'Good.'

'It is sufficient. You may go.'

'All right,' I say, feeling myself being dragged into a gluey kind of stasis. 'I will go now.'

She gestures through the curtains. 'Yes,' she says, 'you may do so,' and I push my way through, feeling the gluey impact of the curtains as they fall on me. For the second time I fear deceit, wondering whether she truly awaits me behind those curtains or whether it is merely dreams, some Oplaus epiphany of the spirit back there to cast myself back over and again upon myself, nothing ever to be changed . . . but I will not allow such cheap depression to possess me. I will not allow it to be so at all; she has been there in the past, she will be there now; and so I prod myself through the clinging, porous silk and find myself in yet another long hallway, dark, dark except for the pool of light filtering from a room on the left, and I walk toward that light, fascinated. Insects like pellets rush like blood through that circle, just as my own blood is charging dimly at me, and mindlessly I walk through that door; see the woman lying naked on the bed, her arms in a languorous posture of crucifixion, dangling toward the floor, her eyes fixed

86

on the ceiling and burning, burning; her breasts flat, falling like teardrops to the sides of her, those nipples sores at the center. My Queen of the Night revealed again to me.

Inside, I allow the transparent curtains which cover the room to fall, and look down upon her. Her little eyes look at me but once, taking me in, and then close once again; she seems to be deeply within some private place where I cannot touch her, yet which is the source of all her response. Some engine room of the spirit. My Queen of the Night. 'It's me,' I say.

'I know that.'

'Do you know who I am?'

'Does it make any difference? All of you are the same.'

'Yes.'

'You are who you think you are. And I am the Queen of the Night, the Queen of the Night.'

'Oh yes,' I say, and my erection is upon me, 'oh yes you are,' and begin clumsily to undress. My hands are shaking; my breath stretches unevenly from the tube of my throat. My clothing falls in heavy clumps to the floor like squat pellets, and then I feel the chill sliding like smoke through the open panels of the body, her breasts glinting at me, deadly in their aspect, needful in their alignment, and I come to the floor beside her, feeling with a finger the cool slab of her skin. 'Yes,' I say again.

'Get in there.'

'I will,' I will, 'I will.'

'Get in there now. I want you to get inside me.' Her legs flex; I catch a whiff from her vagina, steamed dead meats swirling. 'Get in there quickly.'

'Wait,' I say, 'wait,' but she reaches toward me, seizes me behind the shoulders, and unwillingly I insert myself. The heat from her body infuses to mine, spreading dully.

'You are cold,' she says. 'You are very cold.'

The voice simulates affection but when I look at her there is nothing but dead stupefaction, a willingness to please. I must accept. I must accept what has happened here. I am lying with a whore; there is nothing to be made beyond this reality, and shame fills me, the shame only further igniting the lust, which is, of course, the definition of degradation. 'So cold,' she says, 'so very cold.'

'I have come through the Transporter,' I say. 'It sucks the heat from you.'

87

'I know nothing about the Transporter. I know nothing about how you came here.' Her hands are on me like knives.

And it is true. In this room where she dwells the Transporter is foreign. She has no more idea of it than I would of the mysteries of her interior. Creatures entwined together, we share nothing but our humanity, and only barely that; our conjunction is more a matter of accident than otherwise. 'Warm,' she says to me, 'now I feel that you're beginning to get warm.'

Into the fresh, stone slab of her body I go, imagining that I am entering not only her but all of Trinidad, that kind, cruel, busy place where nothing matters but this simple exchange. In its churches and whores there is a kind of simplicity; I have tried both: I cannot deny their effects. Nor their complicity, for I feel that they are the same, Ignition begins within, that slow and painful ignition coming not from the groin, which would be simple, which I could accomplish myself in my own cubicle and without resort to conjoint, but rather from the center, something which vaults me out of myself and which I can find only in intercourse itself. It is this, time and again, that sends me into that vault which I enter, the warmth coming from the center: all things now – the brain, the damaged heart, even the genitals themselves – merely appendages to that basic fire.

I take myself to be in some perilously intimate relationship with her. She is no longer a prostitute but a companion, someone with whom I would spend a life, someone with whom I would Final Trip if that option were left to me. She is the world, I revolving upon her and underneath; from a far distance, I hear her grunts and groans beginning. Synthetic as they may be, they manage to increase my excitement.

I am quite beyond speech. Locked within, trapped within her no less than I am trapped within the cave of my life, I find that I am already beginning to sprout within, sprout and spout and so on, I begin to discharge within her yards of seed, seed and need, need being the seed, and it is this errand, nothing else, which has taken me through the terrifying Transporter and into Trinidad.

I might indeed have accomplished the errand with my hand in my cubicle, might have done it quickly and cheaply and been gone with it, free to devote my full attention back to the necessities of the day . . . but knowing that I have disassembled myself, hurled four thousand miles for this, is not depressing; rather it is an assertion of triumph. It has truly been a mighty errand: what a mighty need it must have been after all to have carried me so far for this purpose! And so I pump and pump, jamming myself into the bed, feeling her body become so insubstantial in my battering that she is merely a plank, an interposition between my body and the bed. I feel her turn watery underneath me; it is as if she is only a means for me to discharge into the bed. I stammer, mutter, moan unspeakable secrets into the flat surfaces of the sheet as I pass them mixed with drool like sputum, and the seizure goes on for a long time; it goes on for a very long time, but finally it is over, that great bark of the body, sneeze of the soul, and on all levels I can feel myself retracting. I have become porous again. Winds pass through me; I have lost solidity.

She lies underneath me crying, and I know that it has been no deception, and that through all of this she has been feeling too. Something.

V

But the deaths are clean, they are pure abstraction, they are unrevealed; and it is possible to believe that they do not exist. They only occur to the uncommitted, those under twenty-five, and only there in the vast, segregated complexes which are their segregated quarters until they are broken out into the various larger complexes where they will live the rest of their lives. Dance. Barker. Baker. Ball. The Province. In these complexes the uncommitted live from their tenth to their twenty-fifth, and it would be possible to believe, for shifts upon shifts, that they do not exist at all, so insulated are we from their presence, so isolated are they, but then again working in the Department forces a shocking sense of contact, and I cannot be unaware that two-thirds to three-quarters, in some of the complexes far more than three-quarters, are suiciding out, as is their option, rather than face on the obligations of the committed. In sectors like Dance it has been known to approach, at times, nine-tenths. This is well known to anyone who would care to study the figures.

But the deaths are aseptic; in a way they cannot be said to exist at all. The important fact is that the suicide rate among the committed has held steadily at one-tenth of one percent or below for as long as figures have been kept. That is the divide, then, the juncture between the uncommitted and the committed, and it is hard to understand why at this time there is interest in understanding the basis of the high suicide rate or what we can possibly learn through detailed examination of a single case in Dance. All cases are individual; each is a mystery; each will tell not about the others, but piece by piece as it is disassembled . . . only about itself.

And yet there is the feeling – Lance has the feeling too and I know this – that there is something about this assignment, something about Jagway himself which will layer upon layer unlock to the core of knowledge and reveal something unspeakable, and that after all of this, none of us will ever be the same again. Hence the holograph, that winking little image, driving through its frozen twitch the one essential message: that they are we, we they, and that ultimately the center has not held.

Something terrible is happening in Dance.

Something terrible is happening within me.

And I am Dance.

VI

Lying beside her then in the aftermath of sex, I feel the empty spaces of her body without lust, enjoying the flesh for merely what it is: the flesh of the female, without desire. Turning slowly as if in a dream, my body feeling vacant, I see that she is looking at me, has reared to an elbow and is staring down with penetration. Her eyes from this aspect are compassionate, compressed to that dark emotion, the eyeballs translucent, and looking into them I can see the blood-network of the retina, the thousand little damages of the body as expressed through the ruptures there, and I think: we are ruined. All of us are ruined; mortality is the first and final blow, the easeful slide to death carried in the rivers of the blood . . . and we have constructed a world which at last understands this and internalizes this knowledge, makes it possible for us not to participate . . . but even that, the freedom from mortality, the control over death by the option to commit it, has not been enough, and we who are the survivors have merely become the victims. That is all.

Death has been turned around so that, for us, life imparts it. She cannot be more than twenty-seven years old, my own age, maybe even a little younger than that, but her body is a ruin, my own infiltration absorbed into that decaying tabernacle. It is too much for me to take, it is too painful; I turn away, unlocking her eyes, and then it is only calm which I feel, the calm and the force of her.

'Are you all right?' she says.

'I'm all right.'

'Tell me that again.'

'I'm all right. I'm all right.'

'Good,' she says and shrugs. 'You have to leave now. I'm sorry, but you can't stay. But I'm glad – '

'I want to be done with it,' I say. 'I want to be finished.'

'You are.'

'Not that. You don't know what I mean. I want to be out of the Department. I do not want to take messages that Lance cannot.'

'Then do it,' she says. 'Do what you want.'

'I am terrified of the Transporter. I am terrified of Dance Complex. Do you understand that? I have seen too much; I do not want to go there.'

'Then don't,' she says. 'Don't go in there. Do what you want.' Her breasts seem smaller and softer. I reach to touch them, but she blocks with an elbow, shrugs me away. 'Not now,' she says. 'That's over for now.'

'I don't want to be part of it. Why do I have to understand? I don't want to. I want to know nothing.'

'Then don't,' she says again. 'Don't do what you dread. You don't have to; it's up to you, isn't it?'

'Sometimes.'

'Everything is your responsibility. Now you can control your life.'

She says nothing; the pause comes over us, aqueous, damp like a cloud in the air, and overtakes feeling. I note that I am shaking. 'Yes,' I say, 'in a way that is true. It *is* true.' I arch my knees, come up to palms, then slowly slide to the sheet. 'I have no choice, you're saying. I have to do what they tell me now that I've elected to live.'

'Yes,' she says, 'but living is not to be unhappy, is it? If it does not make you happy, then why do it at all?'

It is a simple question. I cannot answer it. There is nothing

I can say. 'You'll have to go now,' she says. 'I'm sorry, but you'll have to go.'

'Yes,' I say, and 'yes,' and move slowly upright. Looking at her then, for a moment I think I see something about her that I have never before understood, a hint of grace or composure unacknowledged, but it passes, and with it any feeling of ascension. She is merely a whore in a room in Trinidad. She is merely another unwilling survivor. We look at one another, and in that complex exchange I see everything; not only what has been but what will come next, and there is a vault of pain so great that I do not think I can bear it. Nevertheless I will. One can become accustomed to anything.

'Of course you'll do what you have to do,' she says.

'Of course I will,' I agree with her, putting on my clothing. And I do.

VII

So I go through the Transporter and return to quarters and go over the charts once again (but this time Jagway is not there; there are no images; no one speaks to me), and after a while I fall off to sleep, and the next shift I go off to Dance.

It is obviously pointless to talk to Jagway. Not yet. A proper investigation must move from the outside to the center; it must begin with understanding on the periphery, then move to the middle. So I go to talk to the Group Head from which the information came. After I talk with him, I can then talk to some of the others; eventually the decision will come whether or not I will talk to Jagway himself, but there is time for this. I do not even know if I will attempt to dissuade him. Instructions were unclear on that point.

The Group Head, of course, is terrified that his leakage of information to the Department, although highly proper and part of his responsibility, will be detected by members of the Group; confidence will be ruptured and he will lose his position. Under the regulations, I am given to understand, all Group activities and statements made during them are in confidence, but no one has taken this seriously for a long time, and in a complex like Dance, which has a whole range of illicit behavior, enforcement would be impossible unless the Groups were a funnel of information, of subterranean purpose. For a long time the decisions to suicide have been routinely passed on to the Department by the Group Heads, but never until this time has there been an investigation, a follow-through of any kind, and this is doubtless the source of his terror. He cannot believe my presence.

To a degree I have sympathy with his position, since we are approximately the same age and have the same hideous obligation; it is possible that in his own way the head is closer to me than either of us would ever admit. But this does not change the situation, which is, of course, strongly role-defined. After twenty-five we live within our roles, and often we die of them. *Role is control.* This is a dictum by which all of us must live.

But before the interview, there is the joy of penetrating Dance itself, first the trip through the Transporter, 550 kilometers to the east, jangling and wrangling through the heart of the machinery, the old sweat coating me. Although uses of the Transporter are theoretically unlimited, it is well known that there is an absolute number of trips which one may take before a certain deterioration sets in, and also, trips should not be spaced too closely together because of an exhaustion of the cell-reproduction qualities. Before regulations were created to deal with the problem, a number of cunning types were using excessive Transport to suicide out after the mandatory age of choice, but that was controlled rather quickly through the use of cards and inflexible raw numbers. I am well under the approved limits of use for one of my age; nevertheless, I do not like to enjamb uses, and there is once again that wrenching terror when I commit myself to the machine, that familiar sensation of irreducible loss. There is a moment in which we do not exist; there is a moment in which we inhabit all space and time, and only the instinctive chemistry of the cells carrying its imprint enables us to become what we were, where we want to be. That chemistry is unique and irreducible; therefore the Transporter cannot err . . . but in an infinite universe, there is an infinity of choice, and someone at some time will crawl out of these machines in a different time, a monster.

Out of the Transporter, much shaken, then onto the official landing stage and into the webbing of the complex. Dance is pasted together from three older, pre-ordination cells whose names have now been lost, but the improper amalgamation is still there: streaks in the fusion, a failure of the whole to blend, but, instead, achieving unity only through cross-hatching, odd stops in the corridors, a critical bracing of the frame at certain points. It gives a subliminal impression of ugliness, and ugly as well is the alienness of Dance, an impression that what goes on within these bleak corridors is within a configuration different from my own. Trinidad is not as alien as Dance; the patterns in which they live here are so different from mine that it would take me a generation even to understand their ethos. Ethos, I begin to understand, moving through these corridors, is individual to each complex. Their lives look different from the inside out.

At an opening in one of the hallways a group of them, five or six, all in their late teens to early twenties, are standing around the Transporter, waiting sullenly for the feed mechanism to slide out, as is customary with the older models instead of the smooth, neatly synchronized flow in the larger, newer devices. They look at me with hostility as I pass them, and for an instant I succumb to the unreasonable fear that they are about to stop me, pull me into that hallway and beat me merely for being an interloper, but like almost all of my fears this is without basis; their first appraisal being sufficient, they turn toward one another and look dully at the Transporter. The sounds of conversation are absent; they do not seem to relate to one another but rather might be animals being loaded into a gigantic supply Transporter for movement to one of the stock farms or bins. There is no communication; they are as dull, dumb, bland, unmoving as steers, and for an instant it is I who feel the aggression. I want to stop, turn, shout at them. 'Don't do this!' I want to shriek. 'It doesn't have to be this way. Take charge of your lives, change them, guide them, make them turn!' But of course I do not do this either. No more than they would attack me would I assault them; the limits are quite circumscribed, and we are indeed living in a world without event. I move onward through the corridors toward the near cubicle of the leader, and then, far back, I hear them erupt into conversation and I realize that I have been wrong three times: they would not assault me, they are not dumb, they would not change their lives. They are merely inhabitants of Dance, and I know no more about them, for all their dense familiarity, the familiarity circumscribed on the charts, than I would about the familiar workings of my own doomed organs. I know nothing

whatsoever. All that we are given is the illusion of knowledge.
I go toward the leader.

VIII

'I don't want to discuss it,' he says to me. 'I don't want to
say anything about it at all. I put in the report because that's
procedure, but you're crazy if you think I'm going to go any
further than that. What do you think I am? What do you think
this is? I won't say anything more; I have nothing to add to it.'

And standing there, looking into his face, that stunned face
moving toward blank as he begins to understand the true purpose of my errand, I can see some indication of myself. What
I had been thinking idly has turned out to be true; this is the
man I might have been if I had been raised in Dance rather
than Ego, if I had gone into the unit basis of administration
rather than the organizational. Here, sunk into that face, is
that alternative of myself, living here, working with them, helping Dance to keep up its extraordinary ninety percent suicide
ratio.

Yes, I could have been him, he me; he could have been
pumping whores in Trinidad while I was listening to the strange
music and regarding the holographs as if they would unlock,
piece by piece, the swollen mystery of my own depression to
me. I could have been him and it would have been easy, but
I am not. The difference is slight, but it will hold, and that can
only make our disagreement the more terrible.

Some of this must show. At least a little must have come into
my eyes. He leans forward to partake of it; we catch each other
in a single deep glance, and then his face congests, twitches;
he turns away, looking toward the holographs, and I share that
gaze with him.

One of the holographs catches my eye, strikes me as particularly fine. It shows the Saviour in full projection through a
range of tints; He comes off the cross in an intense act of
accommodation, appearing to be held onto it only tenuously, in
full release floating, taking the full impact of the photographer's
equipment. His eyes open and curiously remote under the hard
bone of the skull, the mouth lurking in a secret quirk that might
have been a smile if there were not so much irony in it, the pain

95

coming upward again then in little ripples and lancing upward to those eyes; somewhere in the deep, trapped center of all this is a hint of obscene laughter, as if His loincloth concealed something which He will not say nor we consider.

Oh, it is marvelous work; nothing cheap about it; probably filmed on the site with models far above the run available for work such as this. The reproduction is excellent; the sincerity of the Saviour shows the actor's skill, and on balance it is an obscene job, bringing home to me for the first time an understanding of why these might be attractive. Although I despise myself, I spot the signs of arousal below; the holograph has touched me – the skin so real, the anguish so deep – and I hurriedly swing my gaze to look at some of the others: a crèche, a John the Baptist, a loaves and fishes, a Barabbas, none of them possessing the effect which this one had upon me. I close my eyes and will my response away; I hope the leader does not see what has happened to me.

But of course he does. How could he not? We are, after all, brothers, acting out alternatives of the same life options. He points at the Crucifixion and says, 'Do you like it? I have many more like that, not for display.'

'I don't like it.'

'Not at all? Not even a little?'

I shake my head. 'It means nothing to me,' I say, but I am betrayed by a subtle quiver of the voice. 'It means nothing,' I say more loudly, and he begins to laugh.

His laughter punctures me; his palms ram up and down his knees as if he were on wire; and, feeling curiously at bay, I stagger back to one of the walls, feeling the stone protrude against me in its rigid cluster. Then, in the center of that laughter, I rebound from the stones and look at him in such a way that he finally stops.

He turns, rubs his hands together, walks away from the holograph and stands against the wall, his back toward me, shaking his head. 'I was only asking,' he says softly.

'Don't ask anything. You're here to divulge information.'

'No. You're here. I'm not here for anything at all except to be left alone.' His voice sounds firmer. 'I will take you at your word. But I will tell you nothing.' He turns back toward me; the laughter is gone. 'Nothing at all,' he says. 'No, you are right.' His eyes avoid the holograph. 'This is quite serious. There is nothing funny about this at all.'

'You have a Jagway under your control who has announced that he is going to suicide.'

'They aren't funny,' he says, looking nervously at the holographs. 'In fact, they're quite terrible. I don't even know why I keep them around. If I had any sense I'd throw them out.'

'When did Jagway announce that intention?'

'No,' he says, still looking at the holographs, 'no, they've got to get out of here. When they start creating laughter, when I think there's something in them to provoke humor, that's when they have to go. You brought it to my attention. I should be grateful for that.'

'Again,' I say and yank him to attention by putting something harsh in my voice, something that one learns from working in the Department but cannot be taught. 'I am asking you about Nicholas Jagway in your group. He has announced an intention to suicide.'

'Well, all right,' he says mildly, 'all right, that much is true. But it's nothing exceptional, is it?'

'That's for us to decide.'

'Four-fifths of them are suiciding out here. Group to Group, the average is almost the same; no leader makes much of a difference.' He shrugs. 'What is there that makes this exceptional?'

'It isn't exceptional. That's precisely the point. You encourage this.'

'Oh no. No, I wouldn't say that. Not that we encourage it, certainly. We never do that. We attempt to dissuade, of course. But it doesn't make much difference. Four-fifths are going to kill themselves.' He coughs into his hand, his shoulders tearing at one another. 'I don't like it. You don't like it. But that's the way that it is.'

'We think you've encouraged this,' I say. It is not the tack that Lance would have me take in this investigation, but I know no other. I can only approach it from the standpoint of trying to define motive. 'In fact, we're pretty sure of this.'

'Well, that's ridiculous,' he says. He turns away, walks toward the opaque window at the end of the cubicle, and leans his forehead against the gelatinous surface, bringing his hands to his chest in an unconscious posture which duplicates the loaves and fishes scene of the holographs. 'That's absolutely ridiculous; you have no right to say that at all.'

'I think we do.'

'We never encourage. On any level we do what we can to dissuade. Suicide is unacceptable; we believe that passionately. But within the strictures of these groups there is so little to do, really, that we can have little effect. You cannot imagine how little latitude we have. You could not conceive – '

'You have enough. Dance suicides are running ninety percent.'

'I wouldn't doubt that.'

'They're only two-thirds throughout the sector, a little less than that over the area. So Dance is running far ahead. Someone has to take responsibility for that.'

'But two-*thirds*!' he says desperately. 'Wouldn't you say this means they feel there are no viable options in the culture? What's the difference between two-thirds and nine-tenths?'

'Twenty-five percent,' I say crisply. 'One-quarter. That's quite a difference. You find one-quarter of the population negligible? We won't have enough to run the machines, to administer the departments. The world will end all right, but it will do so through abandonment.'

'I don't know,' he says. 'I simply don't know about any of that. You do the best you can. What else can you do?' God help me, I believe him. I do not see duplicity in the man who is myself. Nevertheless, it does not enable me to control the fine shaking which has started in the limbs, traversed upward. 'But that changes nothing.'

'What then?'

'Turn over everything,' I say, 'all of the data, all of the material on Jagway, the history of this subject, his background, biography, where his cubicle is located, his plans – '

'No,' he says, 'I can't do that.'

'Yes you can. I come from the capital. You are authorized.'

'I'm sorry,' he says, 'I can't, I won't,' and something comes into his eyes then, some intensity which I can only refract with intensity of my own.

'Confidence,' he says weakly. 'All of us must deal in the strictest of professional confidence. We have become surrogate parents for them; we cannot easily betray . . . ' and his voice wanders off weakly. He shakes his head. He does not seem to be any more convinced of this than I do. 'I believe it!' he says in a different voice, higher, harsher, the sound of an animal deep in his throat. 'If I didn't believe that, I wouldn't have anything, you see. I've got to feel that it makes a difference.'

'Difference,' I say. 'Nothing makes a difference, you fool. Don't you see that? What they tell you they are only telling themselves. It would end the same anyway.'

And, that truth shaken, there seems nothing for the instant to say. Our eyes swing again to the holographs.

For a while we seem to be thinking, my brother and I.

IX

The Saviour stares at me, lunging from His cross, and we exchange a look of deep communion, His agony becoming mine, mine His, the two welded together in a way that speaks deeply to my condition. I can understand, looking into those eyes, the agony that He must have felt, and the anguish is redoubled, because it is not the Saviour but merely a skilled model performing to the instructions of the photographer, the whole of it geometrically rather than artistically patterned, so the effects are gained algebraically rather than through the unconscious. This neither lessens nor eases the impact. It is profound; it goes through: I understand what it must have felt like to be crucified, which, of course, was the only intention the holographer had in mind. Swinging my gaze down the line, I see Him now standing with an ambiguous female figure who might be Mary, might be the Magdalene; hard to tell: the face is posed three-quarters off the line and riddled with a strange blush which distorts those features, muddles them, carries them off-center no less than the Saviour's own gaze, which seems to shift during inspection.

It is brilliant detail work indeed. Really, it is quite extraordinary; the holographer is to be congratulated. Not only is there technical control here, there is reverence and a cunning sense of exactly how that response can best be cajoled. I find my absorption so complete that it is an effort to turn away from it, to see the other man who is also looking at it transfixed. His mouth has come slowly open. He is breathing in shallow fashion. I suspect he is having a response to the structure even more dramatic than my own, and I turn from him then, unwilling to bear witness to this further. 'Do you like it?' he asks. 'Do you like that work?'

'Oh yes,' I say, 'it's remarkable.'

'You really like it, don't you?'

'Yes,' I say, and there is something palpable in the air, something which at a different time I would understand as lust or perversity. I turn from his gaze. I look at the wall, saying nothing now, waiting for his response, and when that response comes, it is as I knew it would have had to be, and no surprise, no surprise whatsoever in any of it.

'I'm glad,' he says; 'you see, I did it. That's my work. It's mine. I did it.'

I turn toward him then and say the only thing I could under the circumstances, magnified because it is the truth. 'That doesn't make any difference at all,' I say.

X

And after a long crumpling instant when he seems to fall in upon himself, he says, 'All right then. All right. I'll turn over everything to you. Everything you want, you can have.'

'That's good,' I say, 'that's very good.' If I turn away and do not look at the holographs he will have no power over me. I have gone to the center of his power now and have found him weak, and now all will be as I want it. 'I'm glad you've decided on that.'

'It doesn't make any difference at all, you know.'

'We've already decided that. I don't think we disagree.'

'They're still going to kill themselves. They're going to Final Trip out here no matter what you do, what anyone does.'

'Let us judge that.'

'They're going to die, all of them, and nothing to be done to stop them, but I'll give you your material. I'll give you what you ask for, you antichrist,' he says, and moves toward a long row of drawers at the opposite side of the room, standing under a simple oil portrait of the Saviour in a benign pose, His eyes glowing with good humor, this representing, it would seem, one of the few good periods in His life. 'I'll give it your way. I'll do any damned thing you want, and the hell with it,' he says and begins to fling open the drawers, bang on them; a little unintentional squeak of pain then as he slams something on himself. Then he has brought out a folder in each hand, stacks them together, squeezes, and, coming forward, smacks them into my hands like dough. Awkwardly I fold fingers over the cold surfaces, bring them against my stomach. There is madness in his gaze. It touches off something within me. I did not come for the folder. It was not only the folder for which I came. And since I began to look at the holographs, understanding their full significance, I have not truly even thought of Jagway.

'Does that give you an excuse?' I say to him. 'Does it?'

The folders delivered, he takes our contact to be at an end, has moved away dreamily, turns now with a start. 'What?' he says. 'What's that? What are you talking about?'

'I said, that gives you an excuse to encourage them, does it? Just because they're going to die anyway? To urge them into suicide, to glamorize and distort suicide and give it the name Final Trip, make it something beautiful for them because you can no longer do it yourself but can do it through a hundred of them, over and again?'

'You're mad,' he says with assurance, 'you're quite mad. I'm diseased but you're insane. Get out of here now. You have what you want; I have nothing more to give you. Get out of my cubicle before it's too late.'

'Too late for what?' I say. 'Too late for what?' and stare then at the Saviour for one more time. For an instant, we seem to exchange mighty and paralyzing winks. *You're right*, He is saying, *you're absolutely right, Jorg*, and it is the first time He has ever spoken to me, and I could not have hoped to hear Him under better circumstances. *You're right*, He says, and there is not only approbation but a glint of humor in what He is saying, a willingness to look backward rather than forward — ironic vision, they call it, a certain *je ne sais quoi* of the spirit. Just be sure this is what you really want, He seems to be saying; it would be dreadful if after having gone through all of this you found that you had made a mistake. If it is what you want, however, go right ahead, go right ahead with it indeed; it will be the best for everyone.

'All right then,' I say, 'I have the chart.' I run my hands over it, feeling a strange, rising warmth coming into the fingers. 'I'll examine it thoroughly.'

'Do anything you want,' he says. 'I don't want to hear from you anymore.'

'But you're going to,' I say. 'You're going to hear from me, and I'm going to hear from you. I want full reports.'

'What?'

'I want you to forward a complete report after every meeting with Jagway from now on.' I reach into a pocket, pass over an identification slip. 'And if you see indication that he is going to suicide immediately, you are to contact me directly through the Transporter.' I pause, evaluate his expression. 'Do you understand that?'

'You're mad,' he says.

'What? What's that?'

'I said it and now I mean it. You're insane.' He looks at the Crucifixion, seems to derive strength from it, looks back at me. 'There's something terribly wrong with you.'

I say nothing, turn toward the door. I am almost there, but his laughter impales me, knifes through in scattering little spikes of pain. 'You believe this stuff,' he says. 'I keep it up there just as a hobby to trap people like you, but you believe it.'

I turn toward him. His expression is implacable. I cannot believe what I have heard. 'What did you say?'

'I said you believe it. You believe that stuff on the wall. You believe,' he says, and his voice cracks; he inhales for control, goes on, 'you believe in some life of the spirit.'

There is really nothing to say. I look at him. From deep inside I feel a cold, murderous spot of purpose beginning to open.

'You,' he says, 'you're going around checking the suicide question. *You!* How are you going to stop anyone from tripping out? You're death himself. You're the Prince of Sleep.'

'Stay away,' I say. I say it not to him so much as to the spot that is flowering, deepening. 'Stay away now.'

'You really look terrible,' he says. 'You'd better get out of here.' His mood shifts. Suddenly there is a horrid solicitousness. Has he detected something? 'Forget what I said. It doesn't mean anything at all. It's just a way that I have of dealing – '

I fold the chart in quarters, put it inside my clothing and walk toward him. It is too late; the spot has swollen, broken. Within me I feel rivers flowing. It was always going to happen. It was going to happen in this way. 'You bastard,' I say. 'You dirty bastard.'

My mouth congests. I can get no more words out. He looks

at me in astonishment as I walk toward the wall, stand in front of the Crucifixion. With all effort I am trying to spit on it, to work saliva into my mouth to defile, but I cannot do it. My mouth is dry, broken. 'You dirty bastard,' I say again. 'I can't stand this anymore.'

I pivot then, turn upon him, and he is standing there, looking at me, only a slight quiver to the hands, otherwise immutable, and I do not know if I can touch him. 'Don't you ever say that again,' I say. 'I never want to hear you say anything like that again.'

'Get out of here,' he says. 'Get out of my cubicle. Get out now. This is where I live. This is my life.'

He starts to close ground, moving toward me, his hands curled into a posture of menace, and for an instant, looking at him, it is as if he is parodying one of his own holographs. Indeed, little flickers of religious passion seem to cross his face. He is transmogrified by that passion, and I wonder absurdly if he was his own model for these postures, if that might not explain everything here . . . but as his stride increases, I see that this does not matter. All that does is that he is going to attack me. *He is going to lay his hands upon me*, and as he raises his hands I begin desperately, clumsily, to fumble within my clothing. 'Don't do that now,' I say to him, babbling, trying to placate, to take his mind off attack while I seize the weapon. 'Don't think of that. Why are you doing this? It won't solve anything,' and I fear for a disastrous instant that I have misplaced the weapon, but no, no, there it comes, moving comfortably, heavily into my hand, the plastic a reassurance, and I show it to him. *Quod erat demonstrandum.* 'Please don't do this,' I say, showing it to him. 'I don't want to hurt you.'

It is impossible that he will go on, understanding what I hold before him, and yet, astoundingly, he does. He has moved either beyond reason or into its center, is so possessed of his purposes that he cannot be dissuaded. 'Please,' I say again, 'please now, don't do this.' It is strange. I am the one who is threatening him and yet my voice is pleading, desperate, as if he, not I, controlled the situation in these spaces, and I understand then that this is true. Only he can decide what will happen next. Choice has been taken from me.

It is inconceivable that I would injure him. I have never used the weapon, have heard only dim reports and rumors of those who have, none of them verified. It is simply an appendage of the job; I cannot imagine using it. But he moves to within a foot of me, stopping only then, and says with a dread certainty, 'You're going to have to kill me now.'

'Stop it. Let me go.'

He shakes his head. His eyes dance with merry light. 'No,' he says, 'no, I won't let you go. You're going to have to kill me to get out of here, or I'll kill you. What do you think of that? You lousy parasite, now you've got to make a choice.'

And he comes at me, hand extended, nails clawing to seize me by the throat, and at that first contact there is understanding, absolute understanding of what he has done to me, what he must have been planning to do from the first, leading me carefully, gracelessly, to this point . . . and for one instant self-preservation and the urge to submit collide within my own perspective, those two beasts rushing at one another. Then I know who I am, what I have been, what I must be, and I pull the trigger.

He staggers back, his posture converted to inattention. I did not want to die. His hand comes toward his forehead, brushes it absently, almost delicately, soothing strands of hair from the small spot that has been opened in the center. If I had wanted to die I would not have waited until this time to allow it to happen. Still standing, almost as if the spot were incidental to this new passion rocking him, his body opens up, the pain-filters destroyed, his eyes curiously shrouded, artful as he looks at me. 'That's it,' he says, 'that's what I was hoping would be. I knew you did not want to die.'

And he falls.

His body uncouples, the joints becoming water, and he slides to his back on the floor, that smile inflating from the corners of his mouth to the center. Little peeps and squawks like those of the synthetics come from him. I fall to my knees, lean across him, and he looks up at me. 'Do you know what you are now?' he asks. 'Do you?'

I shake my head. Unspeaking, I look at the weapon and then put it away, lean forward so that I can hear him tell me what I am. I want to know that desperately; it would be much easier if I knew what I was, because then I might know as well what would happen . . . but he has nothing more to say. He begins to squawk again, the regularity of the sounds a kind of code which if I could only penetrate them might yield the truth . . . but they are impenetrable. Everything is: there are no answers.

104

'Do you understand?' I say to him. 'There are no answers.'

He shakes his head. On the point of inexpressible knowledge he is also in inexpressible pain, the two so welded together that he cannot have the one without the other. Knowing everything now, he can tell me nothing. His frame is jelly. Slowly he dissolves before me.

'I didn't want to do that,' I say. 'I really didn't want to. You made me.'

But I am lying.

After a time I leave him.

XI

After this has been done, the rest is very simple and obvious. Thought is not involved. I no longer have the feeling of being inside myself but am responding to the orders of a very firm and responsible individual who bears some resemblance to but in no way whatsoever is me. I would never have acted so positively, brought the situation to hand. Carrying the chart, I take myself to another part of Dance, where in privacy I review the residences of the other members of the Group. Then I go to the cubicle of the one who is nearest, Sidjo Stammis, to elicit further information about Jagway. I have decided, or the person who is giving me orders seems to have decided, that the proper thing is to elicit as much information about Jagway as I can before I make the direct approach, but when I begin to deal with Stammis I see that I find this oppressive. I do not really seem to be getting anywhere with him, and therefore I decide to use the weapon again, this time on a lower setting. Stammis falls to the floor and lies there in paralysis and I leave him. Surely there will be vast difficulties when reports of these activities find their way back to Lance, as they surely must, but I do not seem to be concerned. Perhaps it is because I have an utter feeling of certainty about all of this. Doubt has been abolished. I know what I have to do now. It is quite simple.

Now it is a matter of intercepting Jagway. The chart, the two interviews yield everything I need to know about him except for one central fact: will he still be alive when I find him? He is indeed; he is in his cubicle, locked over to a catatonic position from which he does not move to greet my entrance into

105

the cubicle, the entrance port swinging, the walls of the space blank, eyes dull and impacted within. He looks at me without knowledge.

'Hello, Nicholas,' I say.

He says nothing, nor does his position alter. Has he already taken a suicidal dose of drugs? This is the thought that hits me, but as I cast frantic glances through the room, finding no evidence, he comes slowly to a standing posture, weaving subtly before me, and says, 'Who are you?' His tone is flat, monolithic, but the words are distinct. He is still able to articulate. He has taken no suicidal dose.

'It doesn't matter who I am,' I say. The chart in the folds of my jacket is heavy. I do not need it. Realizing this suddenly, the folly of it, carrying around his chart when I have already moved into a circumstance where it is of no significance whatsoever, I put it on the floor, step on it heavily, rub my heel into it, and prod the chart into a wall. He looks at me bleakly. I extend a hand. 'Come,' I say.

'What?'

'Come with me,' I say, holding the hand steadily, unwaveringly before me, and he looks at it, his glance wavering from hand to face, his initial fear giving way to a kind of exasperation. He gives no external sign of being a potential suicide; the smooth, blank surfaces of his face are impermeable, implacable, but then again there is no way that the interior can be grasped from a look at their faces. 'Come,' I say again, trying to keep my voice low and level, ultimately reassuring. 'Come now.'

'Get out of here.'

'I'm sorry,' I say. 'I can't get out of here, Nicholas. I can't leave you. It's got to be this way,' and some fact of intensity holds him in place. I can feel the power squeezing out of me in low, deadly pulsations. Again I say, 'Come,' and he holds his ground, then slowly moves toward me.

'I don't know who you are,' he says.

'It doesn't matter.'

'What do you want from me?'

'That doesn't matter either. I want you to come.'

Shockingly he says, 'I wasn't going to do it anyway. I found that out by myself. I want to do it, but I just can't go through. I lied. I lied to them. I lied to myself.'

106

'It doesn't matter,' I say to him again. 'What you did is done; what you didn't do no longer matters.'

'You're from the government.'

'Yes.'

'You're from the capital. I knew they were going to send someone.'

'Don't worry,' I say again. Tenderness squeaks its way through me, emerges in a succession of low, soothing noises. I would never have known that there was such tenderness in me. It is the evisceration of various levels of the personality, a slow unpeeling to find the unsuspected within. Voyage of discovery then to ruined terrain, but one would never have suspected, I would never have known, the shape of those ruins.

Now we stand quietly in the room, our bodies almost bridged by his tentative gesture that comes within an inch of joining, then falls away. An absent tenderness seizes me, an emotion which I find inexplicable in the way it bursts from me unbidden, a part of me that I had never before suspected, as I look at Jagway, at the slant of his face in the darkness, hear the slow rhythm of his breath. I reach into my pocket, take out the holograph and compare his aspect with its design; it is a cunning job, more expert than one would have imagined, an elfin Jagway in my hand. He looks at it and then at me and says, 'That's me. You've got a model of me.'

'That's right.'

'Where did you get it?'

'No matter.'

'I demand to know where you got that.'

'No matter,' I say again, 'no matter,' and something shakes in his control; his hand slips; he has knocked the holograph from my hand. It spins across the room, falls against the wall, shatters. Little splintered pieces of him shower to the floor. Hand to mouth, he backs away from me.

'You shouldn't have done that,' I say. 'You shouldn't have done that.'

He says nothing. His breath has become uneven; I can see its pulsations moving up and down his frame. Now he is terrified, but his terror has given me strength. 'I wish you hadn't done that,' I say again. 'I was merely trying to help you.'

'Get away from me,' he says weakly. 'Get away from me now.'

'I wish you hadn't done that. It would have been easier if you hadn't.'

He has nowhere to go; he is wedged against a wall. I take my weapon from inside of me and show it to him. He looks at it solemnly. I share his gaze, then look up and say, 'You are going to go with me now. One protest and I will use this.'

Once he nods, dumbly, and then he extends his hand. I make the bridging grasp at last, and I lead him from the cubicle slowly, concealing my weapon in the enjambment of bodies so that no one could possibly see it or gauge my purposes.

I had thought there would be response in touching *him*, a feeling which, like my response to the Crucifixion, would have touched *me*, but there is not. There is nothing. I should have suspected that it would be this way. Hardly is it of any significance. We move down the corridors at a good pace, the lights flickering, the corridors empty, and I know that we are coming close now to that sufficiency of all purpose which must have guided me from the outset.

XII

In Madrid I show him the graves of the bullfighters, little gleaming headstones marking the place of relocation. In Cincinnati I show him the place where the nuclear testing device actually struck, burning out the city and everything within five hundred square miles. In Trinidad I drop in quickly, coming just off the landing stage to point out to him the terrain and the place where, five hundred yards from there, the whorehouse is hidden. In Hong Kong we are assaulted by a beggar on the stage itself, crying for just a small contribution to buy him a bit of food, take him out of Hong Kong, but the police instantly seize him and hurl him off the stage, mumbling apologies to us as we vanish. In Toledo I show him the gigantic circular field, ten miles in diameter, under which the machinery beats like a heart, little puffs of wind carrying to us the odor of metal; and in Philadelphia I take him to the Ramp of Iniquity, where for a long, wrenching instant we perform the rites of repentance for the Twenty-Nine Vanquished. Back to Trinidad again, finding it necessary to hold onto him now, wrench him through the Transporter and carry him forward into the maw, and we leap from the stage awkwardly. I begin to drag him forward then to the Church of the Epiphany.

He is weeping. Fear has given way to shock, has now opened to a sentiment which is, regrettably, only for himself. 'It's dangerous,' he is saying, 'it's dangerous to go through the Transporter like this. You can destroy your genes, destroy your brains,' and I say, 'What does that matter? You were going to kill yourself, weren't you?'

'Yes,' he says, looking up at me, face pain-streaked, 'yes I was. *But not this way,*' and it occurs to me that there is an insight here if I really want to grappy for it. It is enough that two-thirds, four-fifths of them are led to suicide; they are entitled, at least, to decide the terms upon which they will die. If they cannot have life, they can at least have a satisfactory death . . . but before I can further ponder this, we are at the church itself, the stone figures of the priests at the entrance, and I pull him through the entryway and into the rear, where I shove him into a pew, sit beside him in the breeze and sounds of the church waiting for an attendant. 'Why?' he asks. 'Why are you doing this to me?' and I look at him quizzically. 'Why are you doing this to me?' he says again, and I can see that he is looking for some kind of answer; that this is not merely astonishment speaking but a genuine curiosity, some involvement in his fate, and I shake my head, say, 'Don't worry about that. You'll find out.'

'We can't go through the Transporter like this. We'll die. There are limits — '

'Don't worry,' I say to him again, 'there are mechanisms to prevent overload. If it would be too dangerous you couldn't leap,' which is a lie of course but a rational one. He looks down at the floor, momentarily too numbed to argue, and one of the priests comes over, carrying the ritual book and a wafer. I raise a hand in dissuasion, trying to indicate to him that we do not wish to participate, merely to witness, but he shakes his head and comes over.

'I'm sorry,' he says, 'you must declare your purposes.'

'We merely wish to witness for a moment.'

'No,' the priest says. He shakes his rotund little head. 'That is impermissible; you must participate in the epiphany; otherwise you have no business being in the church.'

'Bearing witness is legitimate,' I say. 'We are entitled — '

'No,' the priest says. 'Witness may be borne only under the

most unusual circumstances, circumstances for which you have not qualified.' He inclines his head; a flush comes to his cheek. He seems to be overcome by the background, blending into it; then slowly he lifts his head and assumes a different aspect. 'We will have to ask you to leave,' he says.

I point to Jagway, who has been watching this with a stunned aspect, possibly overtaken by the solemnity of the surroundings, perhaps only considering the damage which the Transporter has wreaked upon him. 'This man is a potential suicide,' I say. 'I come on his behalf.'

The priest looks at Jagway and then away from him. 'That is private,' he says. 'That is a temporal issue. We are involved with a different level of meaning here; we are – '

'Remission,' I say then; 'we seek remission on his part.'

'We cannot grant remission.'

'But you can grant the means to it.'

'I don't want remission,' Jagway says. 'I want to leave. I think we should leave – ' and comes crouching from the chair, straightens, the priest looking at him solemnly, and something subtle passes between them, something which I might have hoped for but could not truly define, and Jagway falls back onto the curved, glowing wood. 'Remission,' he says and then puts his face in his hands. 'Yes, that is what we seek.'

'Now,' I say to the priest; 'we will take it now,' and he is confused. I can see disorientation pulsing through his face, a genuine uncertainty. We are left clamped together on the boards, Jagway huddled within himself. I reach inside my pocket, fondle the weapon, feeling once again the glint of the plastic, the precise shape of the barrel. If necessity ever beckoned I would use it, I think . . . but I do not know the level of necessity. The priest returns with another, an elder.

'We understand you want remission,' he says.

'That is correct.'

'A pure and complete remission?'

'Yes,' I say.

'That cannot be routinely granted. In order for you to achieve that, it is necessary for you to seek confession. A full confession of the particulars must be made in which you will make it clear why you are seeking – '

'I will take that consultation.'

'Ah,' the elder says, 'the problem is that such a consultation

110

is not available. It is impossible for the time to be granted now. Also, you are not members.'

'We can circumvent that,' I say. I reach into my pocket, take out credentials, pass them to the elder. 'As you can see,' I say, 'I am authorized.'

He looks at them quickly, then hands them back. 'I am sorry,' he says. 'You are not authorized for confession.' He turns, begins to move away. The priest who had come over to us initially allows for the first time a tentative smile to come upon his mouth.

'As you see,' he says, 'nothing can be done, and therefore you will be forced to leave.' He nods at the elder, who has turned. The elder nods back, makes a gesture, and from an opening high above, near the altar, I see forms beginning to emerge, walk toward us determinedly on the parapet, heading toward the downward ramp.

And what happens next then happens so rapidly that it is hard to fragment it out in mind properly, to reduce it to a series of actions which can somehow be comprehended, but it is not necessary to do this, because at some level I must have, all along, been expecting it to happen, must have seen it happening in no other way: Jagway bolts from the pew, screaming, rears and heads toward the rear of the church, knocking over the priest in his flight, seeking desperate exit; but even as he has moved down the aisle, before he has gone halfway toward the exit, the men on the parapet, some in priestly garb, some of them not, leap from the ramp, plummet, rolling to the aisle, and catch up with him, first two, then a third and fourth conspiring to pull him along the aisle and then to back him against one of the near walls. They do this in silence, not a sound having come since his flight, only the sounds of Jagway's own cries as they cover him with their bodies, and looking at this then I know exactly what is going to happen, must have known it from the beginning, but nevertheless bolt desperately from my position, trying to force my way past the priest. He holds me around the ankles, and the force of my own dive carries me to the ground beneath the pews. We roll and roll then in the little open space, and, grasping him in this involuntary embrace, I have the horrid sensation that I am embracing one of the holographs I have seen in the leader's room, that I myself am being thrown upon an involuntary crucifixion, and I desperately try to rise, to struggle, but am held down by his arms.

111

'No,' the priest says, 'no, you can't do it; you've got to let what must happen be now,' and his voice is so controlled that it might be liturgy which he is reading. Struggles fall away from me. I lie as limp and weakened in his arms then as if I were embracing an icon, and meanwhile Jagway's shrieks begin to bubble away toward emptiness.

'No,' I say then, 'this isn't what I wanted; it wasn't supposed to happen this way,' and make one last effort to disentangle, but cannot do it. I am held firm and the priest says, 'Yes, it is. Yes it is, yes it is, it's exactly what you wanted, it's what you wanted from the first,' and I can no longer struggle, no longer raise myself against him. It is not worth it; it seems meaningless, and so I merely lie there, letting all the sounds and colors wash over me; and for a moment there is a sense of peace so enormous that it is almost dislocating in itself, and in the next moment there is a depression so violent that I do not know if I can deal with it; and so it alternates: peace and depression, depression and peace, flickering away like great spokes of light cast through the church, and in some subterranean corner of the mind at the moment Jagway dies I know that it has happened, and it is at that moment that the long-awaited and promised epiphany itself begins.

PART 3

I

And so it is night, and I dream that I am talking to Gil Orlovitz
(1919–1973) once again, perhaps in a state of dreaming, perhaps waking, one is not sure; night is unjointed as one ages.
'Use artifice,' Orlovitz counsels, 'use artifice, use art, use
masks, the manipulation of masks behind which the truth may
be given, because only the masks are universal, and only the
deceits count.' His face is infinitely weary, filled with infinite
peace. 'You cannot abandon artifice,' he goes on, 'because
that's what happened to all the good ones, finally, a failure of
the ability to detach, a failure of the manipulation: they got
old; they got tired. Irony fell away. The world's madness threw
them into rages, and they wound up freaks and clowns too
decrepit, too unamusing even to exist in the sideshow. You'd
better keep on with the masks,' Orlovitz goes on, and I remember one of the last times I saw him in his apartment in January
or maybe it was February of 1970, smoking cigarette after
cigarette in the black holder that he used to stuff with an unlit
Pall Mall because he did not have the money, he said, to buy
the filters. '*Time* sent up a photographer *and* an interviewer in
1968,' he said, 'and built me up with the idea that they were
going to give my book a really big review, that they were going
to recognize me as an important artist, and then the review

came out, with the picture, and they murdered me, they just tore me to pieces, they just opened me up, and all I want to know is this: Why would they send up a photographer *and* a writer just to destroy me? Does that make any sense? Why would they do it?'

And, I said I didn't know, I didn't know why they would do it. I didn't understand anything about it at all, or why anyone who was sane would want to get into the writing business in the first place; and someone else in the room, someone who was in industry, pointed out to Orlovitz that it was just the breaks of the game, wasn't it? You had to put up with the shit in any job no matter what it was, and he had problems all day, every day like this – sons of bitches out to destroy him. Did Orlovitz think it was any better? And Orlovitz said no, no, there was a level of malice surrounding the so-called creative arts that was not in the business world; maybe it was the marginality, the uselessness of the so-called creative arts that made most of the people criticizing them so inordinately vicious, their feeling being that somehow the artist was getting away with something, making his life out of something that was essentially frivolous, insisting upon a seriousness that was not so; and the businessman said no, he didn't think that would hold up: everybody had problems. Everybody had to deal with the sons of bitches.

And Orlovitz said okay: granted then, writing was a business and business was a business; they both had the same problems, but that didn't mean you had to deal with worse sons of bitches; you weren't entitled to any better than a garment manufacturer or stockbroker, but you weren't supposed to get any worse either, were you? The businessman said no, guess not, just as long as you understood that any man trying to make a living anywhere had these problems, and Orlovitz said okay, guess so; and we had some coffee, and the businessman and his wife left and Orlovitz turned to me and said I lied; don't you think we both lied? If I didn't think there was something better and higher and finer about being a writer than a goddamned businessman I'd give up; of *course* it's better. Of *course* we're doing something more important; and I laughed, we both laughed, with the obscene knowledge of men convinced of secret disreputability, horrid secrets; and I said I had to get going, had to finish a novel the next morning; about fifty pages and it would be done. Maybe three hours. Orlovitz said he wished he had my energy, and I said that I wished *I* had my energy, and we left; and I finished the novel. We saw him months later to celebrate the publication of his second novel in Great Britain and spoke on the phone a lot and he would send me poems. I had lunch with him in February of 1971 to find him possessed with the cheer of the absolute doomed and never saw him again, dropped all contact, and found out in August 1973 that he was dead. The *Times* gave him the lead obituary that day; he would have liked that, also being referred to as a distinguished literary novelist, poet and playwright. And a third or fourth cousin in an article in *The Village Voice* ten days later said that she had never met Gil but had heard of him from the family, who were alternately suspicious and admiring, but as far as she was concerned this proved one thing: perhaps it was better not to be an artist.

I was reminded of something an editor I know once remarked when I said I probably would have a hard time living to the millennium, sixty-one years old then, but would like to make it, really would, wouldn't mind living until 2010 anyway, and she said, 'In 2010, I don't think there are going to be many people around you'd want to know.'

II

But then why sentimentalize Orlovitz, at least to the exclusion of others? Swados is gone and Auden is gone and Berryman and Jarrell are gone too, and although there are an awful lot left, they are beginning to feel and sound like survivors, those who even have voices left anymore, and a good many of them, including the best, the very best, haven't the cunning either to speak well or to keep truly silent.

'Use artifice,' Orlovitz points out. 'Use the masks and let them dance.'

I could have given him filters for his cigarette holder. I could have seen him between February of 1971 and July of 1973, too.

PART 4

I

And so locked to Sherry I rise again, fall again, run my hands over the slab of her body and think: Be cool, Sid, stay cool, be what you can, when you can. She takes me into her darkness, as open to me as ever before, every inch of her an accommodation. I plunge in to climax and fall across her, numb, gasping, slowly receding, while she rubs her hands over the back of my neck and whispers comforts into an ear. You're all right, Sid, you're all right. For all that has happened she is as accommodating as ever. I was a fool to have left her. I will not leave her again. For as long as I have the tenacity I will stay.

Jagway dead, the leader dead, the government man who hurt me, the murderer. More than this I could have known if I had wanted, but I did not want to know; the fact of that murder closed it off for me, and with it a drain of feeling. I cannot care anymore. A new leader, a new cubicle, and in new time a whole set of Final Trips with which to concern myself, bear witness. In the meantime, Sherry. I will take what I can from each moment. I do not think that at the end Jag would have killed himself. If he had, that night in Brooklyn would have ended in a different way.

And I know that I will not Final Trip myself. There is no reason to stay, but there is none to go either; life at whatever level is perversely interesting; it disgorges, piece by piece, miscellaneous hunks of information which if properly understood and balanced may be a metaphor for reality. If I were going to do it I would have done it. I am one of the twenty percent. I am doomed to live.

I lie against Sherry in the spaces underneath the parapet on which we have taken to hide and listen to the cool, cool sound of her breath coming in waves through my ear: magnified, the sound is like a torrent, a torrent plummeting into the pool of consciousness and, cool Sid, I think; cool breath, cool sound, cool soul, cool life . . . while at a great distance the engines continue their grind, and the vise of my life slowly comes in upon me. The dead, celebrated and forgotten alike, are silent.

EPILOGUE

I live on and on in Dance: alive.

AN APPRECIATION

BY JEFF CLARK

'The universe was invented by man in 1976 as a cheap and easy explanation for all of his difficulties in conquering it.'

This statement from *Beyond Apollo* is a kind of challenge: it suggests to the reader that he is here confronted with no ordinary, complacent science fiction writer.

In fact, Barry Malzberg's audience – his supporters more so than his detractors – has been at times hard pressed to assign him a niche within the field. *Final War* was perhaps his first major effort to be published as science fiction, or at least as fantasy, and at that point there was no sweeping the matter under the carpet. The story was (and is) palpable and effective, and an attempt was made to label it (provisionally, one would think) a sort of 'future war' fiction, as suggested by the title. Unfortunately, there is no reference to the future in the course of its text – which can also (it was probably seen and seized upon) make room for something like 'Kafkaesque allegory' in its insistent lap. The best policy is probably not to try pinning the thing down. As the author has remarked in print, he seldom provides a 'means of operation' . . . and this is the main problem that he has represented as a writer within the field.

In spite of this, *Final War* bears many of the hallmarks

which Malzberg's writing has since developed in seizing upon more comfortable science-fictional subject areas. Some of the things that make his style highly distinctive are deceptively superficial in nature: the lengths to which he can run a sentence without using commas (or, in the really long sprints, periods); his very proper syntactical constructs – rigid, hard-surfaced; and the increased weight such conditions lend to his liberally applied vernacular phrases, and even figures of speech. These qualities are evident in *Final War*; also apparent is the difference in his storytelling technique. Unlike the majority of his fellow writers, Malzberg is not 'action-oriented'. But neither does he build sturdy characters within a 'classical' narrative line; instead, he is more often concerned with state of mind. *Final War* offers us three vantage points on an intolerably stagnant situation – through the figures of Hastings, the new Captain, and the First Sergeant – and there is inevitably not much difference between them. These characters occupy three separate positions within the single problem which contains them all, a senseless and endless war action, and their repetitive flutterings toward personal gesture are stifled by this condition of existence. 'Indeed, everything has become the same, as is common now in cases of great tensions occurring under stress situations . . . *now there is no difference.*' So Hastings tells us; and this is an observation that remains pertinent to Malzberg's later, more involved work.

Final War was termed 'too grimly realistic' on one of its rejection slips. But the point at which it touches the heart of a real matter is not one of naturalism, of empirical surface textures. That is not within the author's style or concerns, which are considerably more involuted. The actual character of Malzberg's work and why it is most often compatible with science fiction are matters I hope to determine here, having used this 'war story' as a sort of springboard.

The body of fiction focusing on astronauts and the space program – a large part of which is encompassed by *Universe Day* and the novels *The Falling Astronauts* and *Beyond Apollo* – offers the clearest manifestation of where the author's primary talents reside. This subject area brings within range the two basic aspects of the technology that so fully occupies him: the actual machinery itself, and its seemingly inevitable fleshly concomitant, bureaucracy. Together they re-form the problematical matrix, once represented by the war situation, which can dissolve into solution human autonomy and sensitivity.

But this material offers far greater possibilities of expression. Two important features of Malzberg's style are given a new resonance: its concrete, sensual detail countered by rather abstract, cerebral metaphor; on combination they suffuse the dreaming patterns of flesh and steel which form the corridors of the astronautical novels. We encounter in these books a total immersion in the interior of a single character's mind. In *The Falling Astronauts*, Richard Martin is a man trying to work his way out of a rather linear maze, going from point to point and grasping at pieces of his life and dreams as they fall away from reach. Harry Evans in *Beyond Apollo* is confronted with a more multidimensional maze which he explores on paper, and the fantastic aspect of his experiences is not at all easily distinguishable.

Both protagonists are in desperate situations. The use of the present tense – which Malzberg has employed almost exclusively in recent years – increases the urgency, the inertial flow of the prose, and suggests a mentality adrift. Human relationships are fractional, distorted: they are alternately, and often simultaneously, both vague and threatening, physically and mentally. Just as there is no real and balanced world in these fictions, there are no real and balanced subsidiary characters either; these people are more like vivid nodes on each protagonist's consciousness, perhaps obstacles to be dealt with – analyzed, and if necessary, surmounted.

This matter of objects and analysis is important. Malzberg's central characters are quite mad in ways that usually involve paranoia, obsession; and we encounter each of them in the process of realizing that he is unable to cope with life. He examines each specimen of his world as it confronts him, with what appears to be great methodology, but doesn't know whether his solution lies in basics or abstracts, in encounters or speculations or dreams as parables. There is a tendency to hang hope for illumination upon people or isolated events which cannot really bear the weight of significance bestowed upon them. The entire thrust of a Malzbergean drama is not toward human action *per se*, but toward reaction and the definition of a problem, which may enable the protagonist to come to grips with it – though his failure to do so is usually terminal.

But this last point must be qualified in certain fictional cases. If it sounds like a fixed pattern, it is in a sense ritual. Quite often a narrative structure of minor revelation and overt apocalypse is employed. Each longer work brings its character repeatedly to the brink of revelation, only to have it vanish from touch at the last moment. Personal apocalypse appears often; it can be found variously in *Overlay*, *Revelations*, *Herovit's World*, *The Men Inside*, and especially *The Falling Astronauts*. I have said that the author's people fail to come to grips with their situation, in many of these cases until the last moment, at which time they recognize at last its crushing magnitude even as they are being swept away by it. There is no avoiding the consequences; every game is serious, even Harry Evans's cryptograms, which, though not apocalyptic, are at the root of his dilemma.

And so, on into the nature of the Malzbergean character's problem: it is true that he cannot cope, but this is because he has been divorced from his emotional core, and is nevertheless trying to wend his way toward it by oblique and tortuous routes. The astronaut's life seems to offer the most vivid perspective on this: he wanders amongst scientific abstractions in a bureaucratic medium; his approach is desultorily intellectual – the 'spirit of rational inquiry' – and, attempting to view things in this way, he uncovers ever-multiplying ramifications. He is dissociated:

> I have a wife. Evans has a wife. Evans and I are the same person, but it is easier sometimes to slip into a more objective tense; there is now so little of myself I can bear that perhaps distancing is the answer. Another name for this, the institutional personnel hint, is dissociation reaction. I have a dissociation reaction. Evans has a dissociation reaction. Each of us has a dissociation reaction, but mine is stronger than his. (*Beyond Apollo*)

The deadpan humor makes a point. Every infrequent usage of a psychological term or diagnosis reinforces the impression of a dismissal of their inherent value: the terminology is another part of the machinery; it offers the 'easy answers' (so desirable) halfway to the roots. The emotional answers lie buried within the individual, and the method to all this sullen madness is to demonstrate that the mind, with all its associative cross references, can take one only so far toward revelation and understanding – precisely because it is not a machine, nor connected to one.

Therefore, when the complications collapse of their own

weight, they are often personally devastating. Witness the terrifying moral righteousness of Richard Martin's apocalypse as he suddenly urges an unbalanced astronaut to drop his atomic payload on Earth. In a long, final passage the moment is extended, in a catch of the mental breath which expands the event with an almost objective, dispassionate perspective; this is the culmination of all that has occurred to the 'monkey' who 'got himself cracked open'. Harry Evans does not receive an exit so distinguished: he reaches the end of the line only to realize that he is fatally destined to repeat his course in grim and funny variations.

It is this 'repeating of the course' which is so central to Malzberg's work. There is an overwhelming impression of organic, almost haphazard growth in his fiction, an inertia that permits no return to origins but is urged on by the ubiquitous present tense. His books are in a way test patterns, attempts to complete a circuit from alternative moments (always an *in medias res*, different yet just the same), using the avenues which present themselves with every new effort. Within this circuitry resides the sought-after 'sense of connection', which the author's readers will recognize as one of his recurrent phrases.

So there seems good reason for the ritualistic flavor of his work. It suggests a sort of cerebral incantation on the part of uneasy technological man in order to achieve something that simply cannot be had with the means and circumstances he finds himself possessed of. And the effectiveness of such work is largely due to its being cast as science fiction. This form seems to encourage and enhance the quality of mental process Malzberg illuminates: that ability of the mind to abstract, to synthesize, and to grasp for the meaningful in so doing – constructing the while its own reality.

This is not to say that as science fiction his writing does not evidence more substantially the relationship between man and science, and technology. Malzberg knows, through the conviction of his work and perhaps better than most other writers in this field, that 'science' (whether in jargon psychological, technological, or purely theoretical) does not really explain the Final Cause of anything – for there is no 'perfect knowledge' in it – but only offers useful descriptions of the way things seem to happen. And they are useful *observations* to the degree that they are regularized and systematized – and do not

125

partake of the personal and unnecessarily subjective.

Scientific order often borrows from human order. However, attempting to establish convenience and efficiency in the reverse direction (most obviously, to incorporate the human into technological patterns) can raise that sort of confusion which causes Richard Martin to merge copulation with docking maneuvers in his mind's eye. It is crucial that one of the consistent areas of concern in Malzberg's fiction is sex: it is an act both spontaneous (intimate, sensual) and inescapably mechanical at the same time; striving for oneness and yet self-consciously incomplete. This conflict is reflected and explored by Malzberg, again and again, in a prose that is more fruitful by far than dry discourse.

Even his most hostile and cursory readers admit his power; it is tied up with the things Harry Evans cannot bear to regard, the things which involve himself. One does not have to agree entirely with Malzberg's pessimistic view to recognize that there are problems in any technologized world, and that he has been fingering them luxuriously. If he seems often a better spokesman for science fiction's anti-technology faction than many of its prosaically experimental members, it is that he is more in touch with the abrasive *sense* of the human/technological interface, and that (equally important) his effect as a writer is not at all tied up with ideology (genuine or bogus).

But the questions he poses have no easy answers, just as science has no ultimate truth. Harry Evans discovers this in *Beyond Apollo*, that his cryptograms have no definitive solution, only variations. He does not 'know the language to teach' the authorities. Perhaps the most significant fact to be garnered from his experience is not what actually happened on the disastrous Venus mission, but that the space program has reduced him to a state of hopeless metaphysics. All that is truly crucial and rich in the novel lives as much in the spaces between the narrative segments as within them. *Beyond Apollo* is one of those works Joseph Conrad spoke of, in which the meaning is not a kernel within but envelops 'the tale which brought it out only as a glow brings out a haze.' It is possibly Malzberg's finest creation to date – certainly the most fully realized of his astronautical fictions – and, though recognized for its distinctions, has hardly been explored as yet.

Nor, for that matter, have I been able to map the extent of its author's virtues. At present I am largely content to read his work – by no means a wholly pleasant activity. It need not be. If there is one thing that most vitalizes his fiction it is the unity of his vision; and this fact makes it most amenable to C. S. Lewis's (and my) final justification for literature: that it allows us to see through other men's eyes, yet maintain a sort of personal integrity . . . and hence, an appreciative perspective.

The universe was invented to explain the difficulties in conquering it. Perhaps. Barry Malzberg has invented his own to demonstrate why that statement ought to be defended and remembered on occasion. He is not so much concerned with the universe itself as with the difficulties its existence entails.

NEL BESTSELLERS

T035 794	HOW GREEN WAS MY VALLEY	*Richard Llewellyn*	95p
T039 560	I BOUGHT A MOUNTAIN	*Thomas Firbank*	90p
T033 988	IN THE TEETH OF THE EVIDENCE	*Dorothy L. Sayers*	90p
T040 755	THE KING MUST DIE	*Mary Renault*	85p
T038 149	THE CARPETBAGGERS	*Harold Robbins*	£1.50
T040 917	TO SIR WITH LOVE	*E. R. Braithwaite*	75p
T041 719	HOW TO LIVE WITH A NEUROTIC DOG	*Stephen Baker*	75p
T040 925	THE PRIZE	*Irving Wallace*	£1.60
T034 755	THE CITADEL	*A. J. Cronin*	£1.10
T042 189	STRANGER IN A STRANGE LAND	*Robert Heinlein*	£1.25
T037 673	BABY & CHILD CARE	*Dr Benjamin Spock*	£1.50
T037 053	79 PARK AVENUE	*Harold Robbins*	£1.25
T035 697	DUNE	*Frank Herbert*	£1.25
T035 832	THE MOON IS A HARSH MISTRESS	*Robert Heinlein*	£1.00
T040 933	THE SEVEN MINUTES	*Irving Wallace*	£1.50
T038 130	THE INHERITORS	*Harold Robbins*	£1.25
T035 689	RICH MAN, POOR MAN	*Irwin Shaw*	£1.50
T037 134	EDGE 27: DEATH DRIVE	*George G. Gilman*	75p
T037 541	DEVIL'S GUARD	*Robert Elford*	£1.25
T042 774	THE RATS	*James Herbert*	80p
T042 340	CARRIE	*Stephen King*	80p
T042 782	THE FOG	*James Herbert*	90p
T033 740	THE MIXED BLESSING	*Helen Van Slyke*	£1.25
T037 061	BLOOD AND MONEY	*Thomas Thompson*	£1.50

NEL P.O. BOX 11, FALMOUTH TR10 9EN, CORNWALL

Postage charge:
U.K. Customers. Please allow 22p for the first book plus 10p per copy for each additional book ordered to a maximum charge of 92p to cover the cost of postage and packing.

B.F.P.O. & Eire. Please allow 22p for the first book plus 10p per copy for the next 6 books, thereafter 4p per book.

Overseas Customers. Please allow 30p for the first book plus 10p per copy for each additional book.

Please send cheque or postal order (no currency).

Name ....

Address ....

....

Title ....

While every effort is made to keep prices steady, it is sometimes necessary to increase prices at short notice. New English Library reserve the right to show on covers and charge new retail prices which may differ from those advertised in the text or elsewhere.